Fifty-Fifty O'Brien

SELECTED FICTION WORKS BY
L. RON HUBBARD

FANTASY
The Case of the Friendly Corpse

Death's Deputy

Fear

The Ghoul

The Indigestible Triton

Slaves of Sleep & The Masters of Sleep

Typewriter in the Sky

The Ultimate Adventure

SCIENCE FICTION
Battlefield Earth

The Conquest of Space

The End Is Not Yet

Final Blackout

The Kilkenny Cats

The Kingslayer

The Mission Earth Dekalogy*

Ole Doc Methuselah

To the Stars

ADVENTURE
The Hell Job series

WESTERN
Buckskin Brigades

Empty Saddles

Guns of Mark Jardine

Hot Lead Payoff

A full list of L. Ron Hubbard's
novellas and short stories is provided at the back.

*Dekalogy—a group of ten volumes

L. RON HUBBARD

Fifty-Fifty O'Brien

GALAXY
PRESS

Published by
Galaxy Press, LLC
7051 Hollywood Boulevard, Suite 200
Hollywood, CA 90028

Printed in the United States of America.

ISBN-10 1-59212-362-7
ISBN-13 978-1-59212-362-9

Library of Congress Control Number: 2007903623

Contents

Stories from Pulp Fiction's Golden Age

A ND it *was* a golden age.
The 1930s and 1940s were a vibrant, seminal time for a gigantic audience of eager readers, probably the largest per capita audience of readers in American history. The magazine racks were chock-full of publications with ragged trims, garish cover art, cheap brown pulp paper, low cover prices—and the most excitement you could hold in your hands.

"Pulp" magazines, named for their rough-cut, pulpwood paper, were a vehicle for more amazing tales than Scheherazade could have told in a million and one nights. Set apart from higher-class "slick" magazines, printed on fancy glossy paper with quality artwork and superior production values, the pulps were for the "rest of us," adventure story after adventure story for people who liked to *read*. Pulp fiction authors were no-holds-barred entertainers—real storytellers. They were more interested in a thrilling plot twist, a horrific villain or a white-knuckle adventure than they were in lavish prose or convoluted metaphors.

The sheer volume of tales released during this wondrous golden age remains unmatched in any other period of literary history—hundreds of thousands of published stories in over nine hundred different magazines. Some titles lasted only an issue or two; many magazines succumbed to paper shortages during World War II, while others endured for decades yet. Pulp fiction remains as a treasure trove of stories you can read, stories you can love, stories you can remember. The stories were driven by plot and character, with grand heroes, terrible villains, beautiful damsels (often in distress), diabolical plots, amazing places, breathless romances. The readers wanted to be taken beyond the mundane, to live adventures far removed from their ordinary lives—and the pulps rarely failed to deliver.

In that regard, pulp fiction stands in the tradition of all memorable literature. For as history has shown, good stories are much more than fancy prose. William Shakespeare, Charles Dickens, Jules Verne, Alexandre Dumas—many of the greatest literary figures wrote their fiction for the readers, not simply literary colleagues and academic admirers. And writers for pulp magazines were no exception. These publications reached an audience that dwarfed the circulations of today's short story magazines. Issues of the pulps were scooped up and read by over thirty million avid readers each month.

Because pulp fiction writers were often paid no more than a cent a word, they had to become prolific or starve. They also had to write aggressively. As Richard Kyle, publisher and editor of *Argosy*, the first and most long-lived of the pulps, so pointedly explained: "The pulp magazine writers, the best of them, worked for markets that did not write for critics or attempt to satisfy timid advertisers. Not having to answer to anyone other than their readers, they wrote about human beings on the edges of the unknown, in those new lands the future would explore. They wrote for what we would become, not for what we had already been."

Some of the more lasting names that graced the pulps include H. P. Lovecraft, Edgar Rice Burroughs, Robert E. Howard, Max Brand, Louis L'Amour, Elmore Leonard, Dashiell Hammett, Raymond Chandler, Erle Stanley Gardner, John D. MacDonald, Ray Bradbury, Isaac Asimov, Robert Heinlein—and, of course, L. Ron Hubbard.

In a word, he was among the most prolific and popular writers of the era. He was also the most enduring—hence this series—and certainly among the most legendary. It all began only months after he first tried his hand at fiction, with L. Ron Hubbard tales appearing in *Thrilling Adventures, Argosy, Five-Novels Monthly, Detective Fiction Weekly, Top-Notch, Texas Ranger, War Birds, Western Stories,* even *Romantic Range.* He could write on any subject, in any genre, from jungle explorers to deep-sea divers, from G-men and gangsters, cowboys and flying aces to mountain climbers, hard-boiled detectives and spies. But he really began to shine when he turned his talent to science fiction and fantasy of which he authored nearly fifty novels or novelettes to forever change the shape of those genres.

Following in the tradition of such famed authors as Herman Melville, Mark Twain, Jack London and Ernest Hemingway, Ron Hubbard actually lived adventures that his own characters would have admired—as an ethnologist among primitive tribes, as prospector and engineer in hostile climes, as a captain of vessels on four oceans. He even wrote a series of articles for *Argosy,* called "Hell Job," in which he lived and told of the most dangerous professions a man could put his hand to.

Finally, and just for good measure, he was also an accomplished photographer, artist, filmmaker, musician and educator. But he was first and foremost a *writer,* and that's the L. Ron Hubbard we come to know through the pages of this volume.

This library of Stories from the Golden Age presents the best of L. Ron Hubbard's fiction from the heyday of storytelling, the Golden Age of the pulp magazines. In these eighty volumes, readers are treated to a full banquet of 153 stories, a kaleidoscope of tales representing every imaginable genre: science fiction, fantasy, western, mystery, thriller, horror, even romance—action of all kinds and in all places.

Because the pulps themselves were printed on such inexpensive paper with high acid content, issues were not meant to endure. As the years go by, the original issues of every pulp from *Argosy* through *Zeppelin Stories* continue crumbling into brittle, brown dust. This library preserves the L. Ron Hubbard tales from that era, presented with a distinctive look that brings back the nostalgic flavor of those times.

L. Ron Hubbard's Stories from the Golden Age has something for every taste, every reader. These tales will return you to a time when fiction was good clean entertainment and the most fun a kid could have on a rainy afternoon or the best thing an adult could enjoy after a long day at work.

Pick up a volume, and remember what reading is supposed to be all about. Remember curling up with a *great story.*

—Kevin J. Anderson

KEVIN J. ANDERSON *is the author of more than ninety critically acclaimed works of speculative fiction, including The Saga of Seven Suns, the continuation of the Dune Chronicles with Brian Herbert, and his* New York Times *bestselling novelization of L. Ron Hubbard's* Ai! Pedrito!

Fifty-Fifty O'Brien

Fifty-Fifty O'Brien

THE coaster dip roared like HE shells in a barrage. The merry-go-round wheezed and banged soulfully and the cymbals clanged and the horns blazed away and the horses went up and down and the kids shouted.

The freak show barker delivered his hoarsely nasal spiel, never varying, never ending. The popcorn seller bawled his wares and the peanut roaster squealed with a shrill monotony which went through your head like a knife.

People shouted, people laughed. The hum of the midway went on and on, its pulsation an electric shock which made you breathe hard with excitement. The roulette wheels whirred and the trained seal barked.

And above it and through it went the *yap, yap, yap* of .22 rifles, hammering away with gusto at the mechanical ducks which swam and dived, and dived and swam, on their endless chain. Water geysered, bells clanged, lead whacked through clothespins, splinters sang.

And behind the cartridge-covered counter, on the muzzle side of the chained rifles, stood a young man with straw-colored hair and eyes that flared like gaslights. He was yelling to be heard above the racket, above the clang, above the showering tinkle of empties. He was hazy in the smoke and dust, but his voice was sharp and clear.

3

"C'mon, step right up and winnah a ceegah. Winnah a ceegah. Winnah baybee dawl. Two bits for fifteen shots. Heresya your chance. Heresyachance. Anybodeee can do it. Right this way, step right up."

Over and over. *Crack, crack, crack. Clang clang.* And the ducks and rabbits jumped up and went down, over and over again.

From the next booth, the grifter leaned out and yelled, "Hey, Win! Hear ya leavin' us."

"Yeah. Gonna join the Marines."

"Whatsa matter? Doncha like it?"

"Wanta see some excitement for a change, thasall."

Crack, crack, crack, the pungent smell of smokeless powder and dust and the buzz and clang and clatter of the crowd, the merry-go-round, the coaster dip, the people, the radios, the people, and *crack, crack, crack* . . .

Silence.

Nothing moved.

Brooding, festering jungle steamed unheard as it had for centuries. Vast, empty silence like a wall which roared and roared and hurt your ears. Tense, festering jungle–nothing else.

For a long while Winchester Remington Smith had been standing at the top of the trail, staring down through the twilight tunnel which was the trail. His sodden khaki, mud-spattered and torn, blended in with the tan and red of the muck in the path. His campaigner was faded, wavy from rain and sun, and his leggings were the color of Nicaragua.

Somewhere ahead he had heard a sound. Ten minutes ago he had heard it. And he stood there, waiting, ears smarting with silence. In his hat he carried a few sheets of onionskin paper—orders for Company K. And the paper had to get through.

To push back that still wall which pressed in against him, he muttered, "The only difference between me and a telephone wire is that they patch a wire and bury a runner."

Bitterness marred his voice. For three months he had been at it—carrying orders, stamping alone across mountains, through angry yellow streams, down steep-sided, silent ravines.

And he was under orders to avoid trouble, to get his messages through.

But God, what a relief it would have been to send Springfield lead into a goonie's guts. Sometimes, when he crept alone through the sullen night, he almost went mad with the desire to fire a clip at the silence. Anything to break the tension before the tension broke him.

Perhaps, this time, when he got back to Company K, the top kick would let him stay around long enough to get himself back again. But Company K hardly knew him, and neither did "Fifty-Fifty" O'Brien, first-sergeant USMC. And if Fifty-Fifty O'Brien didn't even see him, then what chance did a fellow have in getting a break?

Fifty-Fifty O'Brien. He'd like to know that man. Fifty-Fifty O'Brien was solid. He didn't let a thing like silence get him. Fifty-Fifty O'Brien was the toughest man in the regiment. Self-reliant, big-jawed, swashbuckling, with a killer's eyes—pale, icy eyes that stared straight through you and out the other side and saw something you couldn't see.

Fifty-Fifty O'Brien and his small black horse—the only black pony in the regiment—were always found in unexpected places. O'Brien had the idea that he himself could bring this guerrilla war to an end.

A faraway click of a hoof, faint in all this stillness, came again to Win Smith's ears. He moved the rifle a fraction of an inch, glanced down to make certain that the safety was off.

His pale, haggard eyes bored down through the leafy tunnel, and he crouched a little forward, waiting for he knew not what. The fact that something besides himself was moving in this vastness heartened him, made him forget the silence for a moment. Something was moving in the steamy heat and silence and it might spell danger.

He could hear the hoofs more distinctly, he could even see a shadow moving through the patterns of sun upon the path. Then he wanted to shout with relief. A black pony was coming toward him—and a black pony meant O'Brien. Maybe he'd have company during the last ten miles.

He started to call out a greeting, but the word clung in his throat, a sodden lump. O'Brien was not on the horse. The rider wore a straw hat, a ragged white shirt, a pair of leather puttees.

A goonie! On the black horse!

Where was O'Brien?

A creak of leather and a startled wheeze from the pony, a swift white flash of amazed eyes, the blur of a hand moving to the boot for a mountain gun.

Win Smith dropped down and the shot screamed over his

head. The rifle jolted his shoulder, shaking the jungle with its crash.

The native jerked in the saddle, clawed at the horn, and came sliding out. The black horse, nostrils flared, charged up the trail toward Win Smith. He snatched at the bridle, caught it, and dragged the pony to a snorting stop.

Very slowly, very watchfully, he went down the red clay path toward the sprawled lump of white. For an instant he was afraid he had missed and killed the native, but the pale flicker of an eyelid gave him assurance. He knelt down and propped the goonie up against a tree trunk.

"What's the idea?" said Win Smith. "*¿Que pasó?*"

"*¡Yanqui!*" spat the goonie in a spray of blood.

"*¿De donde viene el caballo?*" demanded Smith. "And where is the *yanqui* who rode it?"

The sullen brown jaw was tightly set, the eyes were flaring with anger. "*¿Quién sabe?*"

"You know and you're going to tell me about it. If you don't, I'll . . . I'll . . ." He felt in the pockets of his soggy shirt and found a box of matches. He struck one and looked at the goonie's feet. Then he knelt and began to remove a muddy leather puttee.

"No!" screamed the native. "No! I have heard what you do. I know you would torture me."

"That's better," said Smith and put the matches back in his pocket. "Where is this *yanqui*?"

"We wounded him. He is now on his way to our camp."

"What for?"

"He knows much, he is a great man. We would break him

7

with certain means and obtain much knowledge. I went to bring other men."

"Which trail?" said Smith.

"One kilometer back, the trail to the left. But," added the goonie with a sick smile, "they have gone far, you can do nothing."

Smith stood up and looked back along the path. The native was right. He could do nothing about it now. In fact, it would be better if he did nothing. His orders were to the point. He had to avoid any such trouble. The orders were more important than a single man. The best he could do would be to tell them at camp and let the patrol take care of it.

But it was ten miles to Company K and in the meanwhile . . .

"One kilometer," said Smith. "I can see their tracks, anyway. I can make sure. . . ."

Fifty-Fifty O'Brien, the self-reliant, the swashbuckling O'Brien, caught like a rabbit in a snare. O'Brien was too swell a guy to leave in a spot like that.

"One kilometer?" He took out a cigarette, shoved it in the native's mouth and lit it for him. Then, looking down into the puzzled brown eyes, he added, "They'll be finding you soon enough. You won't bleed to death."

He swung up on the black pony and went on down through the sun patterns which leaked into the dense tunnel. He wasn't listening to the nerve-twisting silence now. He had something else to think about.

He found the trail, found the tracks. Several ponies had passed that way at a walk. He put a fresh clip in his Springfield and whipped up the black horse and left his own trail.

The path led into a country cut and slashed by ravines, the

forerunners of the Yuloc Mountains. As it went gradually up, the vegetation became less thick, the trees bigger and further apart.

An hour and a half later, he slowed the black pony's pace and began to look ahead each time he went over a canyon edge. And then, about five hundred yards away, he caught sight of white dots moving along a ravine bottom.

The trail there was long and straight, and from his position high above, Smith could command the entire length.

He dismounted and spread himself out on top of a limestone boulder. He adjusted his sling with neat precision, as though he was again on the firing line winning his expert rating all over again.

Seven white dots, he counted. One horse seemed to have no rider, until he made out the khaki lump which was draped like a meal sack over the saddle. If that was O'Brien, the man might well be dead.

He could almost hear the whir of the chain taking the ducks along their ledge. He could almost hear the *crack, crack, crack* of yapping .22s and the clang of the bells and the whistle and thump of bullets. He grinned down the sights and squeezed carefully.

A white duck pitched over on its side and out of sight. Another threw up its arms and toppled backward. The echo of the shots roared and pounded through the close canyon walls and the reports were curiously hollow out in the open this way.

Another mechanical duck jolted, almost fell, and then clung hard to a terror-stricken horse and bolted out of sight, just as though the duck was alive.

He grinned down the sights and squeezed carefully.

The remaining white dots did not wait to look back. They loosened the horse they led, and with quirts cracking against lathered flanks, fled out of sight into the brush. The sack of meal hung listlessly from the saddle, arms dangling as the mount danced about, lead rope tangled in its forefeet.

Win Smith swung onto his horse and with a hard slap, sent the animal plunging down the steep side and racing along the trail toward the released pony.

It did not take him long to get there. It did not take him long to unsnarl the rope and quiet the rearing horse. He was scared by the listless waving of O'Brien's arms, by the small trickle of red which ran down out of the sleeve and dripped from the stubby fingers.

A pipe-barreled mountain rifle snapped peevishly from the brush. Smith grabbed O'Brien's shoulder and shook it.

O'Brien's eyes flickered for an instant and then opened wide. "Beat it," snapped O'Brien with odd intensity. "Beat it."

"Hey, it's me, Win Smith. It's me, Top. You're okay."

"Beat it," cried O'Brien.

Delirious, decided Win Smith and immediately swung up on the black horse and led the other pony away from there at a swift pace. The mountain guns began to roar and crack down the trail. Powder music. Slugs spanged and howled away from rocks and trees. Win Smith grinned happily, and remained erect in his saddle.

The clatter of the pans in the galley, the rattle of mess kits and dixies, the slamming of aluminum beaten to the off-key song about Lulu teaching a baby to swim, filled the velvety darkness which had dropped over the camp of Company K.

Clinging to the hillside by its tent pegs, Company K was busy finishing its supper in a bedlam which was sweet to Win Smith's silence-stung ears. Confident in the sentries, Win Smith could almost forget that still jungle and the men who scuttled like the lizards through the brush.

"That was hot going, baby," said the corporal on Smith's right. "I hear you popped off three of them."

"Naw, just two. One rode off with the others." Smith was not looking at the corporal's eyes. Smith was looking at the two stripes which graced the corporal's arm. He had just realized something.

After that trick, O'Brien might rate him. Smith began to grin. He hadn't thought about it before, but if they made him a corporal, maybe he wouldn't have to listen to silence anymore. Those stripes were mighty nice looking, too.

"He's gotta idea," said the corporal, speaking of O'Brien, "that the sooner we clean 'em up, the sooner we get out of this stinking mess. Maybe he's right, but you can't tell O'Brien nothin'. Fool trick to go off by himself that way. Of course he got bunged up. He was damned lucky you saw his nag and followed him up."

A man in khaki with a small red cross on his sleeve slid into the circle and sat down on an empty ammunition case. "You Smith?" he said.

"Yeah."

The corpsman nodded. "Thought you might like to know

12

O'Brien is okay. You couldn't kill that tough egg. Y'know what he did? Tried to knock me down and leave the shack. Said he wasn't going to have no damned gob messing over him. I used up a bottle of iodine on him for that crack. One in the shoulder, another in the leg. No bones broke. He's acting pretty mad about something."

"Of course he is," said the corporal. "Y'ever see a top kicker that wasn't mad about something? Gets himself picked off by the rebels and has to be rescued. You expect he'd be singing about it?"

The corpsman looked long at Smith and then quietly went to work on his mulligan.

Four days later, Winchester Remington Smith was still in camp, a fact which set well with him. But, on that fatal fourth day, at ten o'clock in the morning, when he found himself facing the captain and the lieutenant and the patched-up O'Brien, he was very startled.

O'Brien's ice eyes were fixed balefully upon him. O'Brien's left hand dangled in a sling. O'Brien was using a crutch to stand, having refused the canvas chair.

The captain, clean and hard of face, with a great show of unconcern, said, "I suppose this is a deck court, Smith. For conduct to the prejudice of good order and discipline."

"Yes sir," said Smith, avoiding O'Brien's hard glance.

"In a way you have disobeyed your orders. In carrying dispatches destined for Company K, under orders to avoid any difficulties which might lead to the loss of those dispatches, you deliberately set yourself out of your way to track down an uncertain lead which, with a great deal of luck, brought you to O'Brien."

"But . . . what could I do, sir?" said Smith.

"You should have come in, delivered your dispatches, and we could have sent out the patrol. Tracks do not fade that fast. For myself . . . well, I appreciate your feelings in the matter, but the sergeant here has, after all, discipline to maintain. Supposing we put this matter down in the book, Smith, and if, when we get outside, the sergeant still insists, we'll write it into your record. That will be all, Smith."

"Yes sir," said Smith and saluted before he realized that he held his hat in his left hand. In great confusion, he about-faced and marched out of the tent.

He did not stop walking until he had placed several trees between himself and the captain. Then he halted and looked out at the valley below, a stunned expression on his face.

When he had been standing there several minutes, he heard the thump of a crutch coming up behind him.

"Listen, you," said O'Brien, his jaw set and his jowls shaking, "you think you got away with it that time, but I'm sick of seeing a goldbrick around here, get it?"

Smith said nothing.

"The shavetail's got some stuff that needs taking to a *Guardia* outfit over by Mount Pelo. Go get it."

Smith's face came alive. "Mount Pelo? I thought you sent all that stuff back to PC and had it dropped there by plane. No runner can get through to Pelo."

"Oh, so that's it. Now you're telling me how to run the

company, huh? You think you're going to go around shooting off that big face of yours just because you made a grandstand play, huh? I said there's some stuff for Mount Pelo. Go get it and fast, or by God, I'll knock your face through the back of your head and kick your laces up around your neck. Beat it."

Smith looked at the sergeant's slung arm and the crutch and then at the anger which leaped out of the set face. "What's the matter?"

"Plenty's the matter, you damned boot. You think you can get maybe a stripe or two for pulling that boner out on the trail, do you? You think maybe I'm supposed to overlook disobedience to orders, do you? Insubordination, that's what it is. Insubordination! You think by pulling what you did you ought to have medals pinned on you, maybe—nice, shiny medals all over that stove-in chest of yours.

"Well, there ain't any medals in this outfit for the bird that disobeys his orders. What if you'd been killed coming out there, huh?

"I think you was trying to get killed just for spite. And then what would have happened, huh? The goonies would have taken those dispatches and we'd be in a hell of a shape, we would. You're a runner, not a goddam Red Cross dog, and the quicker you get it, the better off you'll be.

"Trying to pull a hero stunt. What the hell do you think you're in? The Girl Reserves? Why, I've got a notion to bash in your grinning, ugly face for you, you mother loving, baby snatching, perverted son. Now get out of my sight. Get out of my sight! Get those papers and get the hell out of camp. I don't care if there *are* goonies on that trail. I don't care if you have to wade in blankety-blank-blank up to your neck, get to Mount Pelo and get back, and by God if you get yourself bumped off I'll knock a hole through you a cat could jump through. Now get out!"

Smith's fists relaxed at his sides. Smith turned and went away. After all, you don't hit a wounded man and you don't hit the O'Briens of the corps.

When he had received the orders and when he had filled his bandolier out of a broken ammunition case, he saw the corpsman looking at him from the front of the sick bay. The corpsman was smiling in a knowing way.

"Where bound?" asked the corpsman.

"Mount Pelo."

"Wheeooo! Been no runners over that way for weeks. Well, I wish you luck, leatherneck. I wish you luck."

Silence.

A bush moved slowly against the wind. From under the branches peered a pair of tired blue eyes under the crumpled brim of a campaigner. Far out across the bleached grass of the plain reared the unshorn head of Mount Pelo, a shaggy sentinel hazy in the heat waves.

Win Smith hitched his Springfield up beside him just in case anything might move in all that expanse. He remained hidden for some minutes with the ringing silence weighing him down.

In two days he had traveled far, mostly by darkness, and the jungle trail had resounded at times with the plodding hoofs of tired native mounts and with the subdued chatter of the goonies moving restlessly through the mountains, bent on some errand Win Smith could not define. Many grimy shirts had passed through his ready sights, but he had held his fire, knowing that even the immense relief a shot would give him would, at the same time, betray the fact that a runner was near at hand to be hunted down.

Something was doing here, and the sooner he reached Mount Pelo, the better. There, at least, he could rest and eat in the company of the two *Guardia* officers.

Assured that he alone moved through the heat, he raised up and started across the plain. His pace was fast and his light pack bounced against his already raw shoulders.

Neguas, those insistent fleas which burrow into feet and lay their sacs of eggs, made walking a painful thing. For lack of attention, the sores were growing. Every few hours he had had to stop to remove blood-gorged ticks from beneath his leggings.

Mount Pelo sprawled out before him. On the northern slope he would find the outfit, if the outfit was still there.

A mountain gun cracked far to the right. A geyser of tan dust spouted in the path before him. Win Smith changed his course, increased his pace, and headed doggedly for his goal.

A second shot bullwhipped from the edge of the woods. Again he changed his course, getting as far as possible into the open.

He had made three hundred yards when he heard the rattle of hoofs on the trail behind him. He whirled and threw himself down into the dust, twisting about and staring back, rifle propped on one elbow, finger tensing on the trigger.

Two horsemen were charging at him, hat brims pressed back, legs jerking as they thumped bare heels into their ponies' sides. Smith aimed carefully and squeezed. The first rider went down in a skidding swirl of dust. Smith fired again. The second threw up his arms; his mount whirled and plunged back toward the woods, dragging the bouncing body by the foot.

Smith got up and faced Pelo, breaking into a jog trot. He had the uncomfortable sensation of eyes staring at him from cover, and he knew that men had picked up his tracks. If they guessed that he was a courier, they would be waiting for him on the return trip.

An hour later, drenched with muddy sweat, he came to a halt before a low tent pitched at the side of a rude, sunburned parade ground.

A man in Marine uniform came out, a weary but immaculate man who bore the silver triangle of the *Guardia* on his hat. Surprise flickered for a moment on his face.

"Where the hell did you come from?"

Smith grinned. "From Company K."

"What the hell? They've been sending their stuff over by PC and plane. Didn't you have trouble getting through?"

"A little. There seems to be something up." Smith handed the slips of onionskin over to the *Guardia* captain.

The captain loosed an oath which would have done credit to Fifty-Fifty O'Brien. "We're to fall back. What the hell?"

"Don't ask me," said Smith, bold with weariness. "I'm just the messenger boy around here."

The *Guardia* captain looked at him for several seconds, observing the muddy, ripped condition of the clothes, noting the absence of a clip in the bandolier, seeing the red veins in the haggard eyes.

"I meant," said the captain, almost losing his gunnery-sergeant gruffness, "that this is funny. They tell me the post is in danger and we're too far out. They tell me to fall back toward the PC. What the hell do they know about it? Sergeant Mallory and I don't have to depend upon guesses. We've got plenty of boys here that know all the answers.

"It isn't this outfit that's in danger, dammit, it's Company K. And the fools had you come through all that just to give me a couple screwy commands. What do they do down there? Cork off?

"But," he added, rubbing his raw beef jaw judicially, "if they say move back, my people move back, and that's that. But Pelo, damn her hide, won't be easy to take again.

"See here, soldier, tell the cook to shovel you out some chow and then pipe down for some snores. You'll go back with us, of course."

Win Smith looked at this gunnery sergeant of the corps, this captain of the *Guardia,* and thought about another man like him—Fifty-Fifty O'Brien. The sensible thing to do would be to follow this gyrene's advice, but a bull-tempered streak in Win Smith made him shake his head.

"O'Brien told me to come back. They'll want to know the score. I'll rest up and leave at dark."

19

"So O'Brien sent you out here, did he? Now tell me what you did to O'Brien."

"I . . . well, I guess I saved his life."

"You saved his life and he sent you out here?"

"Yeah, you see, I shouldn't have taken time to do it. I was carrying dispatch and I wasn't supposed to swing off my course."

"Aw, bunk! That isn't the answer to it."

"Then what is?"

The *Guardia* captain scratched his head in a puzzled way and shrugged. "I dunno. O'Brien is a funny duck—Tough but touchy. See here, soldier, I'm not going to let O'Brien get you bumped. You trail along with us. No use crossing back the way you came. You'd never make it."

"O'Brien said to get back."

"All right, all right. What did he do? Hypnotize you?" He motioned toward the galley and a crowd of dusky *Guardia* men. "Go get what chow and rest you can, you'll need it."

Silence.

A mud-splattered shadow crept up a slippery trail inch by inch, stopping and lying still at intervals. The moonlight lay hazily over the world, painting blue shadows under the rocks and trees. Far over to the right a flicker of red indicated a bandit camp.

For a day and almost two nights, Win Smith had dragged himself down the slopes and through the canyons toward Company K. His khaki was a patch of dirty Irish pennants, the knees of his pants were gone, one legging was absent and his tan tie was torn half in two where he had caught it on a rock.

But it was not this that he minded. It was not that flicker of red. It was not the length of the way. It was the silence, the ringing, never-breaking silence of a brooding, sullen land.

A dogged stubbornness alone drove him on, a wish to show O'Brien that he could get through, that he could follow orders.

But, he thought bitterly, little good that would do him. They'd forget this effort in a day. They'd forget it and send him out again into more silence. And they probably wouldn't even remove that farce deck court from the record.

A hell of a life this was.

How he ached for noise!

Powder music would be sweet, but with it he wanted a merry-go-round going, and a coaster dip roaring, and a nasal voice barking. So this was excitement, was it? Heavy, brute silence that walled you in and thundered in your ears.

Ruefully he remembered how he had stared at that corporal's chevrons that night. He had been willing to give ten to one that he'd be wearing them soon himself—that night.

How the hell did you get ahead in this outfit, anyway? He'd done the thing he thought would be a cinch. Not consciously, but he might as well have done it that way for all the good it did him. You save a guy's life, so he sends you out and hopes you won't come back. Wasn't the bird human? Hadn't he ever heard of a thing called gratitude?

Fifty-Fifty O'Brien, humph. What had been eating him, anyway? Maybe he enjoyed being slung across a horse and carted off to a ceremony called the "cut of the vest."

21

Win Smith went up the trail, groping in the blue whiteness of the night, hoping those goonies would stick to their fire. What if they had a guard along this trail?

But he couldn't leave the trail. Although he was only six or seven miles from Company K, he could not afford to get lost. And you didn't walk straight through that tangle. You had to have machetes to do that.

God, he wished those damned *neguas* would go lay their eggs in some goonie's hide. It might even feel pleasant at first, but when the sores began to spread from the broken sacs . . .

Something moved between him and the moon—a blurry shadow coming down the steep trail.

Smith petrified. He could feel the blood go up to his throat and hammer at his windpipe. It was almost straight down from where he clung to the ravine side. He would have to pass through bright moonlight to go back.

And the native came on, slipping skillfully and quietly over the loose rocks. Smith braced his feet and moved the muzzle of his Springfield up. But he did not quite dare fire. That flicker of red was too close and he was too weary to run far at any speed.

Ten feet, eight feet—he could see the man's eyes, his mouth, the shimmer of moonlight on the machete which banged the white-clad thigh. He could hear the man grunt as he lowered himself down the steep trail.

Five feet, four feet. Smith gripped his stock and lay very still. It was impossible to strike up at the native's head. Maybe . . . maybe . . .

Smith laid the gun aside and reached slowly out with his hands. Seeing something dark move along the ground before him, the goonie paused, muttered something under his breath and, not yet afraid, moved back to better study this thing.

Smith reached out and gripped the bare ankles. The man screamed, snatching at the machete. Smith tried to throw his captive over his head and to the ravine floor below.

Scrambling back, doubled up and clawing at the rocks, the native tried to slash at the unknown shape and hold on at the same time.

Smith reared up and the native jumped straight at him.

They skidded out into space, hit the trail, holding hard to each other. They struck again and fell apart. Smith, with only one thought in his tired head, clutched the native once more as they struck the bottom. The goonie was underneath, lying still.

A hot, salty stickiness ran out from under the woolly hair. Smith fumbled all about him for his rifle. He could hear the calls along the ridge, he could hear the *slap, slap, slap* of bare feet over the path.

He cut his fingers on the sharp lava and knew it not. He banged his head against a boulder and merely shook the sudden dullness out of his brain. He scrambled in a widening circle, striving to find his Springfield.

And then he remembered that he had laid it aside higher up the path. Heedless of the noise he made, he scrambled partway up the trail. The rifle tripped him and he rolled back, clutching its sling.

A large rock offered ready protection from sniping above. He braced himself against the rough face and watched, breathing hard from his struggle and search.

Men stopped against the sky, staring down.

A man called, "*¡Oye! ¿Que pasa?*"

Men muttered to one another for several seconds. Then, "*¡Oye, Ramón! ¿Donde estás?*"

But Ramón was lying quietly in the wash, staring up at the moon, eyes flinty and wide open.

Bare feet pattered briefly, then, "*¡Mira! ¡Mira! ¡Yanquis!*"

Win Smith leaned hard against the boulder, waiting. They had found his hat up there.

Metal clinked, and a creak and snap told of a gun being cocked. But still nothing happened. Smith momentarily considered backtracking, but when he thought of two nights and a day with nothing but silence, and when he remembered that horses could catch him easily enough, he pressed against the boulder and waited.

In a few moments a light appeared at the top of the trail—a torch. It came through the air like a comet with its trail of sparks and landed in the middle of the wash not ten feet from Ramón, still burning.

They could see the dead man in the glare—and they saw something else.

"*¡Solo!*" It went up with a roar. Shadows danced along the crest. A rifle crashed a ribboned line of sparks. The slug yowled out of the wash like a broken banjo string.

Win Smith watched the flare of powder above him and

thought about a row of gas candles which could be put out with the whisper of a bullet. You got a baybee dawl if you hit fifteen, fifteen.

He began to put out the candles, moving along his boulder to keep them from pulling the same trick. The Springfield's jar was soothing to his weariness, its noise a balm to his silence-outraged ears.

One candle, two candles, three candles—and they didn't light again. One came tumbling over the edge, long and white and screaming. Win Smith knew then that it was steep everywhere but on the trail. That was lucky until they got into the wash some other way.

Rock splinters slashed into his eyes. He wiped his sleeve across his forehead and drew it wetly away. Then he took what remained of his tie and put it about his brow.

How many of the devils were there? That *Guardia* captain had been very, very right. These men were too close to Company K for a holiday. He wondered whether Company K knew it.

Maybe this rifle fire . . . but you don't hear a rifle for six or seven miles in the mountains. Too many walls to block it off.

He moved on down his boulder and discovered it to be longer than he had supposed. The face of the canyon was slanting back, steeper and steeper, until he was shooting almost straight up.

A fist of lead slammed into his arm and sent white lightning ripping through his side. With a sense of relief he saw that the limb still responded to command.

Men were arriving up there—many, many men. Before long they would find their way down, take him on the flank and rear and it would be all over.

What would O'Brien say?

In some ancient period, when the volcanoes had spewed forth their flame-digested rock, a bubble had been left in the ravine side. Now, cut by rain, it was a cave.

Smith looked at it and was afraid that his eyes told him wrong. It was set flat under the cliff edge and was a perfect protection against bullets. He had to cross twenty yards of moonlight to get to it, but then, so would the goonies.

He raised up and snuffed another candle and heard the rifle come clattering down. Then, bent over like a quarterback, he dived toward the natural fort.

Stone splinters cut his ankles. A slug caught in his pack and almost threw him. He slid the last ten feet, heels foremost, and pressed against the back of the cave.

The firing on the cliffs stopped. Voices racketed excitedly. Then there was silence.

Smith laid himself at length in the narrow entrance of his burrow and watched the rocky expanse which went out from him in three-quarters of a circle.

Now what?

The moon was sliding down toward the rim and the blue shadows were growing long across the wash. Smith, numb with exhaustion and feeling lightheaded from his shoulder wound, shook his canteen and heard a few forlorn drops rattle and slosh inside.

A creek was murmuring not thirty yards away. The soft

sound of it made him thirsty, the soft music made him grit his teeth against slumber.

The goonies hadn't forgotten him. They would be back. Then he knew. They were waiting for the few minutes between moonset and sunrise—minutes which would be inky black.

It was cold and he shivered. The rocks were shining with dew. He nodded at the long shadows. When it was dark, he would crawl out and scramble to another position. Perhaps he could even sneak through them and get to Company K.

He began to be anxious about the company. With so many goonies so close, something was in the air. A sudden attack would be murderous, even if it wasn't fatal. Company K ought to know about it. Yes, he'd have to get through and tell them.

Darkness was almost at hand. A rock rolled up on the ravine edge. Something hard crunched before the cave entrance. Instinctively, Smith ducked.

The world turned red and white. The blast was physical in its violence. Fragments spattered like bullets, whistling and screaming as they ricocheted from rock.

Dazed and numb with shock, Smith pried himself away from the ground and stared out at the darkened wash. That had been one of those dynamite bombs. They were dropping them from overhead. They knew he'd try to get out in the dark.

The sides of his neck felt wet, and he discovered that his ears were bleeding. Red lights, big and round, cavorted before his face. His body ached as though he had suffered from a beating with clubs.

Minutes ticked past. He knew he'd have to get out of there.

He summoned every latent ounce of strength and crawled to his knees.

He heard the crunch, and threw himself down again. Once more the world rocked and blazed and shuddered. Flying stone and glass had almost ripped the shirt from his shoulders. He bled from a score of abrasions.

He heard the rolling of rocks after a moment. Men were charging across the open space.

He chunked his rifle into his shoulder and began to shoot. The flare of the powder was like a torch. Men in white were coming on at a fast run.

He sent a clip scattering into the magazine and fired as fast as he could work his bolt, fired by instinct alone, expecting the downward slash of a machete every instant.

The third clip showed a deserted front. Two men were sprawled loosely on the rocks.

Smith wormed back into his cave and pushed gravel up before him to lessen the danger of the next bomb.

How long could he keep that up, he wondered? A lucky missile would, sooner or later, hit the top of the cave, ricochet and drop him.

His ears rang and he had a sweet, salty taste in his mouth. His body felt like unstable mercury. Lights flared before his eyes where he knew no lights should be. He felt suffocated and he could not hear.

A third bomb slapped in front of the cave. Sharp missiles ripped through his shoulders and sliced flesh from his back. The concussion shoved him back a yard. Dizzily, he rose up, fumbling for his bolt, head hanging too heavy to raise.

Drooping there on his hands and knees, he fought a wretched nausea.

A rifle ripped at him from across the stream, a horizontal streamer in the blackness, reflected in the water. He got his left hand off the ground and sank back on his heels. The rifle was too heavy to support and red glare hid the sights.

And they were coming again.

He began to fire, but his shots struck rock not fifteen feet in front of him. The muzzle would not stay up, hands were pulling it down. He slid back and found the cave wall supporting him. Clenching his teeth, he braced the muzzle on his knees and pulled the trigger time after time without seeing whether or not he hit.

Shouts, shots, noise and bedlam. But he felt more than he heard. The blood ran unheeded from his ears and shoulders.

A torch soared, sputtering, and landed in a geyser of sparks just in front of the cave entrance. A bullet hit him in the ribs. He tried to shoot out the torch, but he could not see it. The world swam in a black murk.

Once more the night exploded—sharper this time—and again. The torch blazed and flared and lightning struck again. Win Smith slid silently forward, across his rifle, cheek damply pressed to the cold stock.

He was jolted time after time before he finally awoke, surprised to find that day had come. He was staring down at the trail and he was unable to move. But the jolting continued. Fascinated, he watched the legs of the horse not two feet away from his eyes.

He was riding across a saddle, lashed into place. For a moment he wished that he had been killed back in the cave. Then it would be all over. Now it only had to be done again. The goonies had him.

But no. He could see a horse in front of him—just one horse, no more. And no horse behind him. The one in front was shiny black, and riding erect in the saddle he saw Fifty-Fifty O'Brien.

The top kick did not look back. He was intent upon forcing his pony to its best speed. From his shoulder dangled a musette bag lately filled with hand grenades.

That was all Win Smith could see before the pain in his back pushed him into blackness again.

Then he knew he was lying on a cot without knowing quite how he got there. The corpsman was putting away a hypo needle and stacking up gauze and a long roll of adhesive tape.

"Hello," said the corpsman. "Want anything?"

"Hello, gob," said Smith. "I got back, didn't I?"

"Yeah, thanks to O'Brien."

"What happened?"

"Oh," said the corpsman hazily, "we heard something that sounded like artillery, maybe dynamite bombs, and the guys were all for taking a look-see. But O'Brien got sore as hell when the rest wanted to trail along, and he pegged off alone with a bunch of grenades and an extra horse. He seemed to know all about it. And then he came back with you. That's all I know."

"How am I?"

"Hell, you can't kill a Marine, they're too dumb to die."

A rumble inquired from the doorway, "How is he?"

"Okay," said the corpsman.

O'Brien came in looking somewhat tattered but otherwise very happy. "Howya feelin', kid?"

"Okay," said Smith.

"Look," said the corpsman, "you got a cut on your head, top. You better let me fix it."

"Nuts," said O'Brien. "Listen, kid, I thought you might want to know that I convinced the skipper that you're too valuable a man to let loose in those hills. I told him about the guys you knocked off and he says maybe we can work you up to a gunnery sergeant. Anything I can do?"

Win Smith, beaming but puzzled, shook his head and the top kicker went out singing "Bang Away, Lulu," far out of tune.

"What the hell?" said Smith to the corpsman. "He's gonna rate me. I save him and he sits on me, he saves me and I'm tops. What the hell?"

"You're drawing expert pay, ain't you?" said the corpsman. And then with a wise and twisted smile, he added, "It's the nature of the beast and something else you might call obligation. It's O'Brien's boast that he don't take nothin' off nobody."

"Well, swab my decks," said Smith, "I never thought of that before. I guess," he murmured, "that it would be pretty hard to owe a guy your life."

And he lay back on the cot to marvel, and to drink in the clatter of pans in the galley, the yells from the tents, the tramp of feet, and the strains of "Bang Away, Lulu," pouring raucously forth from the big mouth of Fifty-Fifty O'Brien, the guy who paid his debts.

31

The Adventure of "X"

Chapter One

THE cell stunk of disinfectant and the unwashed bodies of all the drunks. A slit of dirty light struck the end of the wooden bunk, lending a sickly grayness to the enclosure.

The face of Larry Grant was also sickly gray. But for all that it was a well-molded face. The cheekbones were high, the jaw well proportioned, and the blue eyes were alive and intelligent. The rumpled Legion blues did not fit the face. One looked for an officer's cap, a riding crop and polished boots instead of the blankness on the arm which signified a private.

Larry Grant looked across the room at the soggy hulk of Legionnaire Lipinski and drew back his lips from his teeth. "If that fool Sergeant Boch were here now, lord, what I'd do to him."

"Think of his stripes," muttered Lipinski.

"Stripes? Yes, his stripes. But if I were ever to meet that man without his stripes I'd hammer him into so much dirty filth."

"It's a good idea," muttered Lipinski.

"Sure, it's a good idea. What did I do? Nothing! What did he do? He struck me with his stick and slammed me in here." The surge of bitterness in Grant's voice made Lipinski sit up straighter.

"You were out of uniform," stated Lipinski.

"Bah! Out of uniform! What do you fools know about a uniform anyway? Am I supposed to nurse a set of rags like these forever? What a fool I was to ever set foot in this outfit!"

"Now you're here, you've got to soldier," said Lipinski.

"Soldier? What the hell do you know about soldiering? If I had that man here, right here between my two hands, I'd throttle him until—"

Something rattled outside the door. Both men whirled, facing the grate. A big jaw was there—a pair of close-set eyes. Sergeant Boch surveyed them very coolly.

"So," he rumbled. "Legionnaire Grant would like to throttle me, eh? He'd like me between his two hands, *hein?*" With a kick he sent the cell door flying open. He strode in, hands on his hips, glaring.

Grant sat where he was and said nothing. Boch closed the door, locked it and threw the key into the corridor. Then he took off his tunic and tossed that through the grate. His stick and revolver followed.

"Now, you yellow camel," snarled Boch, "that's Sergeant Boch out there, see? And this in here, this is So-and-so Boch, see? And what are you going to do about it?"

Grant stirred restlessly, his mind flashing out a warning signal to him that this was some kind of trap. He looked at Boch's throbbing neck muscles, at the hard, red face.

"What are you going to do?" thundered Boch.

Grant stood up. He took an uncertain step forward. Lipinski drew in his feet and melted into the wall. Boch's eyes held a flame; his hands were clenching and unclenching. Grant took another step.

Suddenly Boch struck. The smack of the blow was loud in the cell. Boch struck again. Tottering, Grant lashed out with both hands, striving to seize the towering hulk he saw in a blur before him.

But Boch had known what Grant would do. Boch seized the slighter man, gripped his throat and slammed him back against the wall. Savagely, Boch banged Grant's head on stone, time after time. Grant sagged slowly, his eyes rolling white, his knees buckling. A thin course of red went down his neck and disappeared into the uniform collar.

Boch grunted and dropped the limp body. Then he whirled to the door and bellowed: "Corporal of the guard! Come down here with a bucket of water for this cur!"

The corporal came and, a moment later, Grant came uncertainly to, staring up at the raging man above him.

Boch grunted again, reaching out for his tunic and putting it on. "So you're not so tough now, *hein*? Not so tough anymore. I heard what you were saying down here. You won't say it again. No, not ever again. I've got a tasty little detail for you, Legionnaire Grant."

Grant, his whole body a flaming ache, lay still, listening.

"You," continued Boch, "are going out with Muller and his squad—to spot Tuaregs. Intelligence work, *mon brave*. We have ways of ridding ourselves of such as you."

"Intelligence?" said Grant, hoarsely.

"Intelligence," repeated Boch. "You're going down to the Ahaggar Plateau to spot Tuaregs. And I doubt if you'll get back alive when I tip the word to Muller. Now get up! Clean yourself. Be ready to march tonight!"

Boch seized the slighter man, gripped his throat and slammed him back against the wall.

Chapter Two

CRAWLING down through the narrow defile, Larry Grant spat out a mouthful of dust. That ricochet had been close. The snap and scream of bullets bouncing off the rocks over the head of the patrol was far more deafening than the spiteful sniping fire which had been going on for an hour.

Last in line, he could see Muller's back ahead. Muller's back was coarse and the khaki shirt was black with sweat. Muller's tunic was lashed to his pack. The others of that miserable patrol were too far gone to think. They merely crawled and hoped they'd get out alive.

Lord, how far this was from the tan parade grounds of the US Army. For an instant Grant was puzzled. What was he, Lieutenant Stephans, doing here? It was all a nightmare, unreal. He was half minded to stand up. Then a slug spanged close to his head and he groveled lower into the choking dust.

Sergeants! How he hated the beasts. It seemed to Grant that he had spent his life avoiding them, being mauled by them, obeying them: the sergeant he had accidentally shot in the States, the drillmaster at Sidi, and Boch. Now he had to deal with Muller.

Exhausted, half crazed with thirst and hunger, he raised himself to stare again at the back up ahead. Muller was a

39

martinet. Everything was duty. To be slapped about by such a brute of a man seared Grant to the core.

He caught sight of Sam Ying's yellow cheek. Sam Ying crawled in Muller's wake, like a dog. The Chinese was completely subjugated. He was like an automaton. The thought of it made Grant shudder.

Filth, cursed orders, imminent death—Grant had a way of escaping from this. Some night he'd blast out his brains. Or would he? He had too much stage presence to go out that way, acknowledging that sergeants had whipped him. Maybe there was some other method.

His thoughts were hacked off by a flash of white lightning which ripped across his shoulders and hammered him flat into the dust. A small sound escaped his lips and then he compressed them tightly. He was numb, unable to move.

When he could think again, he knew this was his way out. Plugged by Tuareg bullets.

Rustling came to his ears. A rough hand ripped his pack and rifle and tunic away. Muller grunted, pawing at the wound.

"Get up, you *salopard*!" grated Muller. "Get your ugly face out of the dust and crawl. You're not hurt. You've got a scratch a real soldier wouldn't feel."

Grant rolled his eyes back, trying to collect himself. He saw Muller's coarse face through a haze of pain. He could feel the raggedness of the wound. He could feel the blood coursing down inside his shirt.

"Get up," roared Muller. "Want to leave me in the lurch, that it? Trying to get hit on purpose, weren't you? You filthy pig, get up and crawl!"

The flame of rage licked up and devoured the fires of pain which racked Grant.

Slowly, summoning every ounce of nerve, he struggled forward. Muller slammed the rifle across the wound and tightened its sling.

"Damn you," spat Grant.

Muller went back to the head of the small column. He was searching for more rugged terrain where they could stand up and fight the Tuaregs off. If they came to open ground they would have to cross it with Tuareg rifles cutting them down like ducks in a shooting gallery.

Grant crawled in their wake, swallowing their dust, his squinted eyes on the hobnails of the man in front. He was dull from the shock of the bullet. The hot feeling of the blood was terrifying.

He knew that he was not playing a very noble part in all this. The question of his courage did not enter into it at all. He was just a bayonet unit, a private soldier. Once he had been an officer. Once he had been able to hold up his head—but not now.

Thirst tortured him; but he knew better than to drag at his canteen. Thirst would have to be worse before he could do that.

How long had he done this? Hitch, gather himself up and drag. Those Tuaregs had been on their trail since dawn and now it was almost sunset. To make it worse the moon was already up, almost invisible in the onslaught of the sun's scorching rays. There'd be no escape by night.

Presently the column stopped. Grant sank into the dust,

listening to the snap of stray slugs and the undercurrent of Muller's voice.

After a short rest, Grant felt better. The wound was clogging up; the bleeding was stopping by itself. The pain was less. He became enough interested in the proceedings to raise himself very cautiously and stare ahead.

Instantly he knew that their number was up. A flat plain two miles wide was just ahead. They'd have to cross it. The Tuaregs would swoop in upon them and tear them to pieces. This was the end.

Muller was pulling the machine gun from its carrying case. "Attention, you idiots," cried Muller. "Around this point is a small circle of rocks. I'm going to cover your retreat. If any of you get back to base, tell them this."

He stared at their uplifted faces, spat deliberately into the dust, and continued: "The Tuareg tribes are massing for combined resistance to France. But the keynote is a shipment of ammunition which is coming through a pass to the north.

"Guarding that pass is a platoon of the Legion. Their position is a puzzle to the Tuaregs. All of you know the whereabouts of that platoon. Under no circumstances are you to go to it, understand? You will be followed and the platoon will be attacked and the ammunition will get through.

"Get it straight; remember it; and if I don't come through, you know what to tell them at the base. The Tuaregs are massing, waiting for ammunition. The ammunition is holding them up. Ammunition will spring their attack against outposts. Do not go to the platoon. Do you understand?"

All heads bobbed dully. All heads except one: Grant's.

Grant was glaring at Muller with a steady ferocity born of hate, pain and thirst.

Grant smiled bitterly. Muller was making a grandstand play—all for the Legion! Muller had something up his sleeve. Muller would get through all right and the rest would be dead on the plain.

Grant was not entirely sane. His usually intelligent face was a mask. His blue eyes were as hot as a gas flame. Slowly he hitched himself forward.

Muller turned his back, rounded the point of land out of sight. None of the others paid Grant any attention whatever. Their eyes were riveted to the plain. They knew what would await them out there. But the sergeant had said go and they would go.

Grant got to his knees. He jacked a bullet into his gun and followed Muller. Unsteadily, when he was protected by the rocks, he stood up. Muller was selecting his post, scanning the ground about him carefully. When he heard Grant's slow footsteps, he spun about.

Something in Grant's expression warned Muller, but the sergeant snapped: "Get back there, you yellow fool. Get ready to run for your worthless life."

"I'm not running," replied Grant, very distinctly. "You're making a grandstand play, that's all. You're glory-grabbing. You're thinking about medals." His voice was monotonous, ugly. Insanity swam in his eyes.

Muller whipped his revolver out of his belt. "Get back!"

Grant sidestepped swiftly. His gun came up for a smashing stroke. The steel-shod butt crashed into Muller's blue jowl.

Muller went down, heavily. Dust spurted as he hit. Grant lowered his rifle and wiped his sleeve across his eyes. Suddenly he realized what he had done. He had struck a non-com and the *bataillon pénal* would be his lot from now on.

The thought jerked him back into reality. Like a man awaking to find a nightmare real, he looked about him and then back at the sergeant.

No need to blow out his own brains, now. The Tuaregs would attend to that. Grant knew that Muller's strategy had been sound. They'd have to cross the plain. Someone would have to fight a rear action.

He staggered to a rock and sat down. He couldn't return to the Legion—not now. All the bitterness swelled up inside him. A recklessness came with it. In spite of pain and thirst, he laughed. He'd have to shoot the works. And there'd be plenty of sparks when he went out.

The Chinese, Sam Ying, wondering what had happened, peered around the corner. His eyes went big when he saw Muller in the dust.

Grant's voice had a ring and snap it had lacked for months. "Ying! Pick up the sergeant, get the men and run for it. I'm covering your retreat."

The others of the squad came forth, crawling like crabs. Yells were sounding up the ravine. The Tuaregs were not far away. None of the men asked any questions. Casting off the sergeant's pack, they picked him up.

Grant hefted the machine gun. He felt a certain exhilaration—if he lived he'd be sick later, but he doubted that he'd live that long.

The rest of the squad started for the open at a run. Grant watched them go, noted that none of them looked back. Suddenly he wondered if they were worth saving.

Hoofs thundered near at hand. Tuaregs yelled loudly as they sighted their quarry. Grant expected a sleet of bullets to cut the squad to pieces.

But no bullets came—only hoofs and yells.

Chapter Three

A Tuareg, astride a charging black horse, burst into sight. A two-handed sword was held aloft, shattering the rays of the departing sun. The man was veiled, only his eyes showing. The white robe swirled about him.

Behind him came others. Hoofs and yells and the clatter and ring of steel deafened Grant. He waited, holding his fire until the targets were more certain.

The wall of running horses loomed large before the muzzle of the gun. Grant cut loose.

Sitting, he tried to keep the machine gun steady. But it jerked, hammered and rocked about him as though he were a small, roly-poly doll.

The bullets slashed through the Tuaregs, cutting a wide pattern. A horse screamed and reared, spilling its rider out of the saddle and under the hoofs. Another fell, skidding from excess momentum.

The Tuaregs shouted and tried to turn, but others were pressing from the rear. The gun hammered on with its appalling slaughter.

Abruptly the pass cleared. Grant ceased firing. His wounded back ached from the shock of the recoil. He felt a little sick. A horse was striving to raise its head. Grant picked up the gun and put the beast out of its misery.

He saw that the squad was gone, reduced to an occasional sparkle of metal far out on the plain. They would be able to make it now. He wondered what Muller would do when he regained his wits: stamp and swear and vow that he'd get Grant, of course.

But Grant knew there'd be no getting him. When the Tuaregs had succeeded in untangling themselves, they'd come back and kill him. His position was far from satisfactory. His back was exposed as well as his left flank. He couldn't cover three ways at once.

Strangely, none of this seemed to worry him so very much. In spite of pain, the rankling ugliness of his late existence had been wiped away. He'd gotten even with Muller. Of course that still left Boch, and the drillmaster.

The sergeant's pack was close at hand—also his canteen. Grant's own were back up the trail where he had been wounded. Unscrewing the cap, he drank of the liquid. It was hot and metallic, but it helped his throat.

Digging into the compartments of Muller's pack, he found some flinty biscuits and a tin of sausages. With his bayonet he opened the can.

He sat there taking a bite of sausage, a bite of bread and a swallow of water, repeating until nothing was left. He listened intently for the return of the Tuaregs. Of course they'd get him at the finish, but he might as well take a few along to Heaven with him.

For an hour he sat very still, thinking and waiting. The sun went down over the mountain rim and the moon began to turn the world into glossy blue white.

He realized that he was cold. He felt about him for his tunic and then remembered that it had gone with his pack. The sergeant's tunic lay near at hand. He looked at the chevrons and smiled. He donned it, trying not to move his back too much.

When the Tuaregs came back—

A sandal rasped behind him. He whirled, trying to level the rifle. A man in heavy robes sprang at him. Grant grabbed for the throat and his hands tangled in the veil.

Yells broke out on all sides. Suddenly he was drowning in a sea of cloth. A voice was above the rest, crying out orders.

A moment later he stopped struggling. He hadn't intended to go out this way. Probably he'd face torture now.

They pulled him to his feet, holding his arms. A Tuareg in a long blue veil studied him. The Tuareg's eyes were like silver dimes with holes bored in the center.

"A sergeant!" said "Blue Veil."

Grant glanced down at the chevrons and then back at the Tuareg.

"Perhaps you'd like to die now," said Blue Veil in very clipped French. He took a revolver from his belt and juggled it. "Yes, I think you would like to die now."

"Go ahead," replied Grant, unafraid.

Blue Veil put the revolver back in his belt. "But I do not think I will kill you. You are from Intelligence." His eyes stabbed Grant's face. "Yes, Intelligence. We know a great deal. We also have intelligence."

Grant's gaze was steady. His blue eyes were calm.

"And because you are from Intelligence," continued Blue Veil, "perhaps you can buy your life. Where is that patrol?"

Yells broke out on all sides.
Suddenly he was drowning in a sea of cloth.

"What patrol?" said Grant.

"You know what I mean. You French think you are very clever. You think you can guard the pass and keep me from getting ammunition. But I will kill off that platoon."

"I don't know of any platoon," replied Grant.

"You're lying. You know where it is. Tell me and I let you go."

"I don't know where it is," said Grant, doggedly.

Blue Veil laughed derisively. "I know that you do. There are ants here, Sergeant. There are sweets here, Sergeant. Would you like to be tied across an anthill and smeared with honey? A sweet death, but rather painful. Tell me and I let you go."

"I know of no platoon," said Grant.

"You're a stubborn brute." Blue Veil turned his back and snapped orders to his men. For a moment, Grant thought that he was about to receive punishment. Then he saw the Tuaregs haul forth their pack animals from the pass.

Camp was made in a short space of time. Fires were lighted and food was cooked. Grant was seated at the base of the wall, a guard at either elbow.

After he had eaten, Blue Veil squatted down before him. "It is too late to do anything tonight. I keep you under heavy guard. But you could go now if you would tell me."

"I do not know anything to tell you," replied Grant.

Blue Veil stood up. "Bah!" He spat deliberately into Grant's face. "Tomorrow morning you will tell." He turned and entered a tent.

Grant hunched his knees up under his chin and stared at the cooking fire. Blue Veil was wise to postpone this thing

51

until morning. Even a stout heart will go soft if given too much time for thought.

By this time Muller and the rest would be struggling homeward. Or perhaps they would stay for more information. At any event, the word would go through about the uprising.

These Tuaregs were bad medicine. As desert raiders they were under the impression that they ruled the world. No caravan captain would think of venturing forth without a Tuareg guard. If he did, then the Tuaregs would wipe out his command.

Desert racketeers, that's what they were. Ugly devils, spooky in their veils—but every inch soldiers. That was their profession and had been for centuries.

The black guards were silent, staring ahead, hands propped up by their rifles. Grant looked at their hawk profiles. Swell chance he had of getting away. And in the morning—

The platoon would have to succeed in wiping out that ammunition train. If ammunition did come through, there'd be hell to pay in plenty. Grant began to realize just what French control meant in this part of the world. A handful of soldiers policed this district. Things could so easily get out of hand.

Something like *esprit de corps* was born in Grant. This was real. He did not have to take a sergeant's bullying abuse. He was here to think for himself, act for himself—even though death was not far distant.

The glowing fire died to a pile of pulsating red coals. The camp slept.

Chapter Four

IN the silence of a Sahara night, Grant heard voices which had no earthly form. They were the voices of his past, calling to him across oceans and continents and years—a snatch of song, a hearty curse, the brassy blare of a bugle.

How far away it seemed. He squirmed as he thought of the part he had played. The disgrace of that court-martial had only been capped by the disgrace of running away.

His fine, narrow face twitched when memory hit too hard. Pain clouded his eyes. It was his curse to have to think. Where others only acted and realized nothing of their danger, he knew he had to act anyway. He knew fear as does every intelligent man.

Sergeants! Damn the part that they had played. Why hadn't he remembered the things he had heard about the sergeants of the Legion—those towering, awful figures who had to be addressed as "sir"?

As Lieutenant Stephans, he had had nothing to do with sergeants. He had been above them and beyond them. But as Legionnaire Grant—

A chill coursed over him like a bucket of cold water. The desert night was icy. The cooking fire had died. Looking at his guards, he was snapped back into the realness of his danger.

The Tuaregs had bowed their heads over their rifles. Their

breathing was regular. Grant went as taut as a cocked gun. They were asleep!

No, maybe they were shamming. Maybe they wanted him to run so that they could plug him.

Nothing stirred in the camp. Even the horses drowsed after a hard day of riding. Grant moved a little, just to test the guards. Their breathing did not change. Grant moved again.

Suddenly bold, he stood up without touching them. His back was stiff where the bullet had left a furrow. By this time the khaki shirt had frozen into the wound, making an effectual bandage.

Still the sentries did not move. Their heads were pillowed on their hands. Their veils were a filmy cloud behind the vertical stocks of their rifles.

Grant saw his canteen beside the cooking fire. He stepped silently toward it. His revolver was there. Hastily, realizing that this was too good to be true, he shook the canteen and found it half full. Something was wrong. They wouldn't let him get away like this.

The plain stretched out before him, hazy in the moonlight. Grant took a cautious step toward it. Certainly the sentries would awake and plug him. His back crawled, waiting for a bullet.

He took step after step, placing distance between himself and the camp. Looking back he saw that the guards had not moved. Almost out of earshot now, he quickened his pace.

Plotting his position by a star, he headed north. He looked back once more. No sounds of pursuit were to be heard. The coals of the cooking fire were faintly visible like a red eye.

He began to run. The wind was cooling against his face, the plain fled by under his hobnailed boots. He couldn't make for the hills. He'd have to take the middle course and trust to luck. When morning came, he'd be far away.

Until now the thought of his return had not bothered him. He had been too certain of his execution. But now he realized that he was walking straight into the *bataillon pénal*. He'd be a *joyeux* when he got back to the Legion.

He closed his mouth like a trap. This was one time when he'd stay and take his medicine. He'd have to. He'd face Muller's charges and take the rap.

One hour, two hours, and he still headed into the north. By the ragged outline of the mountains around him, he knew exactly where he was. And the knowledge made him stop.

He was heading straight in toward the hidden platoon! But then, that would be his only salvation. Alone out here the Tuaregs would get him again. He'd go up to the pass and surrender himself to the lieutenant there. He'd tell him what he had done and Muller could bring his charges later.

Feeling better in his decision, he slogged toward the range where lay the pass. Some twenty miles beyond the platoon was another post—a squadron assigned to the Legion. He knew it was there. He had seen their two-seaters over the desert on their patrols.

Hours slipped by, and he found himself walking through the blackest night he had ever known. He stumbled into boulders, slid down the sides of hidden washes; but the star kept him on his trail.

The moon was gone and the sun would be there presently.

He hoped he was far enough from the Tuareg encampment to be invisible.

The sun swam up over the mountainous rim of the world, sending shafts of cool light across the plain. It was fresh and invigorating and Grant quickened his pace.

Before long the desert gathered up the heat and threw it back. Heat waves danced along the crests. A mirage came up and disappeared before it was clearly distinguished.

His wound was stinging. He knew he'd have to have medical aid before long. Otherwise infection would overtake him.

He sat down to rest against a large rock, taking advantage of its shadow. He'd wait a while and then go on. He had not realized how tired he was. His eyes were haggard.

Maybe it would have been wiser to have taken to the hills. He looked at the brown jumbles of stone on his left. Instantly he sat up straight.

"My lord, it can't be!"

But it was. A horseman had moved into deeper cover a mile to his left. Grant turned and looked to his right flank. A white robe swirled and disappeared behind a rock.

The Tuaregs were following him!

Then they had let him escape on purpose. But why?

He got up and started north again. Covertly he studied the movements of the raiders on either flank. They were flitting from rock to rock, keeping pace with him, taking advantage of the cover afforded by the hills.

When he got to the platoon— Grant stopped dead and stared into the north. So that was it. The Tuaregs had known he would go to the platoon. And they wanted to know the exact position. If they knew, they would have little trouble ambushing the patrol which kept their ammunition waiting across the mountains.

A tight smile came briefly to his lips. So that was the game, was it? He was a decoy, like a hunter's wooden duck. He was a potential charge of dynamite. But he couldn't stay out here on the desert to be slaughtered. His only salvation lay in reaching that platoon. And if he went there, the platoon's purpose would be defeated and many would die.

His lagging feet took him north again, still toward the patrol. He was unwilling to throw aside this chance at life. The *bataillon pénal* might await him with its living death, but that was better than Tuareg knives.

Besides, what did he care about France, about the Legion, about drill sergeants?

He stopped again, realizing that he did care. His eyes stared longingly at the only refuge. He could not go on toward the aviation drome. The Tuaregs would get him long before he got there.

He had only his revolver for protection and that would avail him little against long-range rifles.

He had no right to jeopardize the lives of the platoon. If he was any kind of a soldier, it would show now.

Abruptly he sat down, drew out his canteen and took a drink. "No," he said in a low voice. "Rabble, perhaps, but they've got more right to live than I have."

He turned and looked to his left. "All right, Blue Veil, come on out here and knock me off. I'm no use to you now." He took another drink on it.

He felt strangely different. Although he did not realize it, he had been questioning his own nerve for months. He had shown to himself, that most critical observer, that he was a man after all.

Maybe when he felt the knives he'd regret it. But then it would be too late. Yes, the patrol had a right to live.

For minutes he did not move. He did not even look north until a flicker and sparkle caught his eye.

He scowled. A flashing dot appeared and reappeared in the mountains ahead of him. Talking sunlight! Heliograph! He felt in that moment like a man who has lost a race. Nevertheless he took out his revolver and noted the message in the sand, writing with the muzzle.

When the dots disappeared, he read his message: "Come right to this dot."

"They've done it," whispered Grant. "They've given themselves away and now all hell can't help them."

He stood up. No use to hold off now. The Tuaregs had seen that beam and the Tuaregs would know what it meant. A swirl of cloth confirmed his observation.

He strode swiftly forward and then broke into a run. He'd have to get there before the Tuaregs did; and he'd have to go some to do it. He might as well save his own neck.

Those fools—that had been a blunder on their part. They had seen him and had sent that message, little knowing what kind of a trap they were springing on themselves.

He came to the base of the mountains. Two men were visible up on a high rock. He would not have seen them at all had it not been for the gold braid of one—the lieutenant, most likely.

Grant scrambled over a pile of stones and started up the slope. He glanced behind him; but he could see nothing of the raiders. The Tuaregs had followed the skirts of the hills, of course. No telling where they were.

Grant stopped and cupped his hands before his face. "Get out of sight! Tuaregs!"

"*Quoi?*" shouted the officer.

"Tuaregs!" cried Grant. He pointed wildly to both sides and the rear.

But his warning was too late. He saw a horseman and the flash of a rifle at the same instant.

As the report echoed hollowly through the ravines, the lieutenant stood up very straight, his hands gripping his throat. He toppled off the rock and crashed into a shale slide. His body stopped an instant after the second shot.

The other man up there strove to jump down, but he was too late. His body jerked and he fell back against his heliograph tripod, knocking it down.

Grant had a hasty glimpse of sergeant's stripes on the dead man's arm. Then Grant sprinted up a small canyon, deeper into the mountains.

Shots cracked behind him. He heard a sharp detonation over his head. Glancing up he saw a kepi and the muzzle of a rifle.

He climbed swiftly, forgetting his back, forgetting everything but the bullets yowling about his flying heels.

*As the report echoed hollowly through the ravines,
the lieutenant stood up very straight,
his hands gripping his throat.*

Strong hands pulled him over the edge of the barricade. He dropped into the rudely constructed compound and stood up, breathing hard.

Some forty Legionnaires were about him. Some of them were already at the wall, firing down into the desert below.

A corporal approached Grant. "Sergeant, I am Corporal Duval. Did you see either the lieutenant or our sergeant out there?"

"Yes," said Grant. "They're both dead."

Duval's weathered face did not change. "Then, Sergeant, as you are the senior officer present, it is up to you to take command."

Grant backed up a pace. His eyes went down to the chevrons on his sleeve. "Command?" he said.

"Yes. What are your orders, sir?"

Chapter Five

GRANT looked about him. He could see the faces of the men who ringed the place. He recognized none of them. He looked back at Duval to make certain that the man was serious.

But Duval was all respect and obedience. The situation was so ludicrous that Grant wanted to laugh. He had come up here expecting to turn himself in for a swift passage to the *bataillon pénal*! But instead he was in command, just because he had been cold and had donned Muller's jacket.

A high rock in the center was used for a lookout post. A Legionnaire called down, "They're massing for a direct attack!"

Legionnaire Grant reverted to Lieutenant Stephans. His face was a disciplined mask. His eyes were sober. "What is the lay of the land, Corporal?"

Duval, heels together, said: "You came up the pass, sir. The Tuaregs can't get us from the rear. We must resist a frontal attack."

"Where are your machine guns?"

"Commanding the pass as it comes down."

"Then," said Grant, "place those guns in such a position as to rake both the pass and the slope before us. You haven't time to worry about the caravan now."

Duval saluted and strode quickly to the waiting gunners. "Take your pieces to the front. Quickly."

The gunners immediately snatched up the tripods and moved them. In less than a minute, the machine guns were slamming short, wicked bursts down the pass into the forming ranks of the raiders.

Grant watched the procedure with a sort of silent awe. He had not actually thought that they would carry out his orders. And yet they had done so absolutely without question.

This was the first time he had ever commanded men under fire. There was little thrill to it. They were all responsive to his order and he felt responsible for their lives. Just because he had happened to have chevrons on his sleeve!

Another corporal came up. "Sir, I am Corporal Schwartz. Does the sergeant wish to check our ammunition and supplies?"

"Your word is good enough," replied Grant. "How long can they last?"

"Not more than twenty-four hours, sir. We've waited for the caravan several days and we're getting pretty low on water and food."

"I don't think the Tuaregs will stay at it very long," said Grant. "Place a guard over the water."

"Yes, sir," said Schwartz, saluting.

Grant pulled his kepi down over his eyes. He felt like a burglar coming in here and bossing these men about. He had no right to do it; but how could he tell them?

He went up to the *murette*. The rock wall had been thrown up hastily for defense. The Legionnaires were half lying against it, firing between breaks in the stone. They glanced up when they sensed his presence and then went on firing.

A pair of field glasses lay in the niche the lieutenant had reserved for himself. Grant picked them up and studied the massing below.

The Tuaregs were gathering out on the plain, evidently preparing for a rush. Blue Veil was behind them, issuing orders.

Grant went back to the center of the compound. Duval came to him and Grant took the man's whistle. He blew "cease firing," and waited for the guns to stop their sharp barking.

His voice was very loud in the ensuing silence. "Wait until the charge has reached the pass mouth. Then, sights two hundred meters and volley fire. Machine guns change for enfilade fire down the slope."

The Legionnaires changed their sights and laid their rifles back along the *murette,* waiting. Once more Grant was jarred by the implicit way they obeyed him. Who was he to be obeyed, anyhow?

He went back to the lieutenant's niche and watched the Tuaregs. The horses were drawn up in ranks. Long rifles and two-handed swords flamed in the sunlight. The mass started ahead at a trot. The pace quickened to a canter. Then at a fast run they catapulted toward the pass. Before they reached it the group broke into two sections, one heading straight up the slope.

With the whistle in his lips, Grant waited. He took down the field glasses to better judge the distance. The veils whipped, robes fluttered, horses reared as they plunged ahead.

Two hundred meters, Grant judged. He blew a single, shrill blast. The guns responded as one rifle. The machine guns clattered, swift and deadly.

The uproar was deafening. Empties spat away from the *murette,* smoking into the compound. The Tuareg yell was thin, lost in the thunder of exploding powder.

The charge came on to a hundred meters. The pass was strewn with kicking horses and shrieking men. Abruptly the lines shattered themselves against an invisible wall. The Tuaregs turned and raced back.

The guns stopped. Legionnaires coolly blew the curling smoke out of their barrels and sat back. Grant exhaled a great sigh. If those rifles had failed to respond when they did, the Tuaregs would have struggled up to engulf them; and that would have been the end. He knew, then, that he had borne all the strain on his own smarting shoulders.

Grant turned and looked up at the rock. "Lookout! Watch for any further movements below and report them instantly."

A thin "Yes, sir," drifted down.

Grant seated himself with his back to the *murette.* He was very, very tired. His wound hurt like hellfire itself. Schwartz came over to him.

"Corporal," said Grant, his haggard face lifted up, "I've been marching all day and all night. After that shambles, the Tuaregs will hold off for a little while. Carry on while I take a nap."

"Yes, sir," said Schwartz with a salute.

After that, Grant dozed. He awakened every time the machine guns started and went to sleep each time they stopped.

He was as nervous as a cat, not because of the Tuaregs, but because of the command.

Just before dark, he made another tour of the defenses. Men looked at him through the red glow of the sunset, speculation in their eyes. He noticed that they talked together in low tones after he had passed.

A chill went through him. Did they suspect his masquerade? After all, he might well be expected to carry the thing off successfully. He lacked nothing by way of knowledge in military matters.

Chapter Six

SOME of his self-reliance had left him when he reached the base of the lookout rock. He stood there glancing about him. Schwartz and Duval and two other corporals came out of the shadows of the *murette* and approached him. Their stride was a little uncertain and they did not look him in the eyes.

Duval came to a full stop before him. "Sergeant, we have been talking it over."

"We are not safe here," added Duval, screwing up his weathered face.

"No," said Schwartz, staring past Grant, "we are not safe here. We think it best that we retreat up the pass under cover of darkness and escape in the direction of the aviation drome."

Emboldened by Grant's silence, Duval stepped a pace forward. "The caravan will know about this. They would not miss the firing. We are going to retreat."

Grant tightened his mouth. "Have you planned all this out?"

"Yes, it will be very simple," said Duval.

Grant looked him in the eye. "So it will be simple, eh?"

"Yes, very simple," echoed Schwartz.

The situation was clear to Grant. The men were growing panicky through inaction and doubt of the Tuareg movements. But if they retreated from this *murette* they might meet the armed caravan which could easily defeat them in the open. For an instant he was panicky himself. He did not know how he could cope with this. What would Muller do? What would Boch do?

Grant stepped forward until less than a foot separated his face from Duval's. "So, you'd turn tail and run, *hein*? You'd turn your back on the enemy? You're yellow!"

Duval faltered. Schwartz flushed angrily. Grant's voice was raw, dripping with venom.

"So you'd run!" roared Grant. "You're a pack of yellow curs!" He snatched Duval's tunic and shook the man. "Do you realize you'd meet the caravan in the pass? Do you know what you're up against? No, you brainless, spineless fish, you wouldn't know.

"I'm here to keep you from getting killed. You're trying to take a fast way out, trying to leave the Legion in the lurch! Do you know what would happen if you ran?

"No, you're too damned witless. The ammunition would get through, understand? It would go through and the Tuaregs would wipe our outposts off the map. I know you don't care about your vermin-chewed hides. But you've got to think about the others.

"Oh, you don't like it? You don't like it. Get back up there on the *murette* and wait for the night attack. Get up there!"

Duval, released, staggered back. His teeth were bared and his fists were clenched. Grant whipped his revolver out of his belt and slapped the butt against Duval's jaw. Duval went down on his knees. Grant kicked him in the side and then swung, raging, on the others. They scurried like paper scraps before the wind. Duval got up shakily, head down, and walked away.

Grant strode to the *murette*. The Legionnaires were facing front. "If any of you want to run like the yellow sheep you are, go on and run! Go on! Get out before I throw you out!"

Not one man moved. Grant, sweating, went back to the lookout rock. He bellowed at the man on watch: "Wake up! Do you see the Tuaregs?"

"They're out front," came the reply. "Milling about like they're waiting to make an attack."

"Well, watch them!"

Grant saw a greasy-haired Italian kneeling at the water casks. He stepped nearer and saw that the man was drinking.

"What the hell are you doing?" cried Grant.

The Italian leaped up, spilling the water from his canteen cup. "I'm the guard, *mon sergent.*"

Grant's fist lashed out and sent the man rolling into the dust. "You're supposed to guard it, not guzzle it. Stand there at attention. Why don't you say something?"

"I—"

"Shut up, nobody asked you to talk."

Grant paced the length of the *murette*. He felt a little nauseated at himself. But then, these men didn't understand anything less. They'd have gotten themselves slaughtered if he hadn't stepped in.

Suddenly he thought about Muller. Muller's words when Grant had been wounded had been of the same timbre.

Grant realized then that he would still be lying in that pass, whipped, if Muller hadn't goaded him on. Muller had made him fighting mad, had made him forget his pain in hate.

It came over Grant in that moment that Muller had done him a favor.

"The Tuaregs are coming!" cried the lookout.

Grant bellowed: "Range two hundred meters. Stand by for the command to fire."

He sprang up on the wall, staring down the pass. The Tuaregs were coming indeed. They seemed as numerous as at first, and twice as angry. They spilled across the plain, headed for the pass. The range narrowed swiftly to two hundred.

"Fire!" cried Grant.

Machine guns started to work like clocks. The barrage of steel jackets slapped into the charging ranks, mowing the men down, dropping the horses, blocking the entrance with the dying.

A loud explosion rocked the earth behind Grant. The Legionnaire below him fell back, an ugly wound at the base of his neck.

Grant stared up. Faces were on the cliff above him. A hand grenade hurtled into the compound and exploded. Two more Legionnaires fell forward.

Grant understood. Under cover of this attack, the Tuaregs had somehow gotten above them. Their position was untenable. He snatched up the rifle of the dead Legionnaire at his side.

Sighting up at the round head against the red sky, he pulled the trigger. The Tuareg pitched forward, falling almost on top of the lookout rock.

Another head appeared. Grant blew it out of sight. A hand grenade came down, exploded in midair. The Legionnaire on watch was blown to pieces at his post.

Grant ran toward the base of the cliff. Duval was in his way and he thrust him to one side. Grant started up the sheer face.

"Wait!" cried Duval. "You can't go. Send Gian!"

Abruptly, Grant remembered that, after all, he was in command here. The Italian was close at his side. Grant pointed up. "I'll cover you. Here's a revolver. Clear that top!"

Gian went up, swift and lithe, sure of himself. Grant stood back and grabbed a private by the shoulder. "Cover that man."

Gian went on up. A head appeared and went out of sight before the shot had ceased to echo from the gun.

Gian clung to the edge of the cliff. The revolver fired once, twice, three times. Gian waved his hand to Grant and started to come down.

Suddenly, seemingly without reason, Gian straightened up and loosed his holds. He turned over as a man does in a back dive. His body lighted a few feet away from Grant. A bullet from out front had done that.

Grant felt a little sick. He had been responsible for that. His order had sent Gian up there to die. With pain in his eyes, Grant turned back to the *murette*.

The machine guns had taken care of the slope. The attack

had been stopped. But in the settling murk of twilight, the Tuaregs were taking up positions closer to the *murette.*

Darkness came in a few minutes and with it came silence. Schwartz approached Grant, saluted smartly. "Sir, do you think there's any chance of getting word to the aviation drome? They could stop that caravan from the air."

"They don't know we're here, do they?" said Grant.

"No, sir. If we could hold out until morning, the planes could finish this up for us."

Grant weighed the possibilities. No man could get through. No man could hike twenty miles through the darkness.

"Where are your flares?" said Grant.

Schwartz thought for a moment. "In the lieutenant's pack, sir."

"And the pack?" said Grant.

"Is with the lieutenant."

Grant scowled. "The lieutenant is down there, dead, right in the thick of those Tuaregs. But if we're going to get out alive, we'll have to have those flares."

Chapter Seven

A T midnight, Grant had made his decision. They would have to get out of there by morning, if they got out at all. They lacked the water to stay. If the aviation drome would send a squadron over at dawn, the caravan could be wiped out and the Tuaregs would run for it.

Grant located Duval. "I am going down for the lieutenant's flares. If I don't come back—"

"Sir," said Duval, "we can't allow you to go down. You would be deserting your command."

Grant's eyes were dangerous. "You can't what?"

"It's too much risk, sir."

"To hell with that," snapped Grant, heading for the *murette*. Duval's hand was on his sleeve, detaining him.

Schwartz and another corporal were there, blocking his way. "You can't do this, sir," said Schwartz. "You're the one who can get us out of this. Call for volunteers."

Grant was about to blast them with searing words when he knew that they were right. He didn't dare go away and leave this post.

"Attention," roared Grant. "I want volunteers to go after the lieutenant's flares."

Silence fell along the *murette*. For a moment it appeared

that none of the men wanted the job, and then five came slowly toward Grant.

He raked them with his eyes. "All five of you can't go." He fumbled in Muller's pockets and found a report book and a pencil. Tearing off five strips of paper, he numbered them. Dumping them into his kepi he passed it around.

Five hands dipped into the cap; five faces were bent over the slips. A small, compact Legionnaire with a very old face stepped out a pace.

"I'm one, sir. When do I go?"

Grant felt the words choke in his throat. "Right now. I want the pack which contains the panels and flares. Without it we can't get out of here alive."

The small Legionnaire saluted and did a smart right-face. He climbed over the top of the *murette* and dropped silently out of sight into the darkness.

Grant paced restlessly back and forth. He listened intently. The entire platoon was listening with him. Would the man get through? Their entire front was blanketed by the Tuaregs. The lieutenant's body lay in the midst of the raiders. It was an impossible task.

Abruptly, shots flashed out in front. A Tuareg yelled loudly. The gun spoke again. The fire doubled instantly.

After that everything was very still.

Grant muttered, "He didn't make it."

A thick-faced man was conjured up before Grant. "My slip said 'two,' sir."

Without waiting for orders, the Legionnaire dropped over

the side of the wall and was gone. Grant's jaw muscles worked nervously. He felt as though he himself were out there, gliding over loose stones, trying to keep away from the Tuaregs and yet reach that precious pack.

Minutes passed, dragging. Grant caught himself holding his breath seconds at a time.

The roar of guns made Grant jump. His fingernails were digging into his palms. Sweat stood out on his forehead. This time there was no reply.

Silence dropped again over the mountains. Grant felt something snap inside him. He stepped ahead, but Duval caught his arm.

An indistinct blur was at his right.

"I'm number three, sir."

"Get the pack," muttered Grant.

Seconds, minutes, silence in front. Grant felt a lump in his throat. He couldn't breathe. He couldn't see. His orders were doing this. Were his orders right? Was this really necessary?

Yes, they had to spot the caravan. They had to signal the drome. Perhaps the drome was waiting for an emergency message.

That man would get through. He had had time. He would make it. He had to; because Grant knew that he didn't have the nerve to send another out. He had never known what it was to hold a man's life in his hand. It took more nerve to give those orders than he had thought he possessed.

A scraping sound came to them, grew louder. Hobnails on stone. The man was making it! He was making it back with the pack. Grant's muscles were as tight as bowstrings. He was mentally pushing the fellow along, straining forward as though that would help.

Suddenly rifles cracked. A small sound came from the other side of the *murette*. A body rolled a little ways; boulders turned; the rifles stopped.

Grant knew he couldn't take the fourth. He didn't have the nerve to send another.

Before hands could bar his way, he was over the *murette* and gone.

He scrambled down the shale, heedless of the noise he made. In the starlight he could see a silent shadow against a rock. That would be the Legionnaire.

Strangely, no one fired at him—not yet. He arrived at the body and knelt. The pack was there. Fumbling for it, he felt the hard glaze of the open eyes. He withdrew his fingers as though he had been stung.

Whirling about, he sprinted up the slope. A rifle slapped a bullet at his heels. Another took it up. Suddenly it seemed as though a thousand guns were pounding at him. But this did not seem to trouble him greatly. It was better to be shot than to order men to their death.

The *murette* was close in front of him. A khaki arm snaked down to grasp his hand and pull him over.

His face went numb. Blinded, he clawed at the rocks before him. Hands grabbed him, pulled him over. He sprawled on the ground, unable to see. Gingerly he touched his face. The cheekbone had been laid wide open by a ricochet. Blood ran hotly down his chest.

His vision cleared and he saw the pack beside him. He stood up and took out the flares and the light pistol. His fingers were greasy with blood, but he would not give the task over to the rest.

Fitting the big shell into the pistol, he cocked it and raised it high over his head. A red light soared far above him and burst in a shower of stars. He discharged another and then another.

Three red lights—that ought to bring them.

He wilted suddenly. He swore at himself for his weakness, but he could not stand. He had been going on nerve too long. The back wound and now this had been too much.

Perhaps, he murmured, hugging the ground, perhaps if he slept a little, he'd— He scarcely knew when they bandaged his face.

Some hours later he opened his eyes and sat up. He was at the base of the watchtower, in its shade. A machine gun was rattling and a loud roaring filled the air. For a moment he did not understand.

Then he saw the planes. Two of them diving and banking higher in the mountains. Each time they came down they fired swift bursts into an invisible target.

The panels were laid out in their black pattern. He knew that one of the corporals had attended to the signaling. They had wanted to leave yesterday. They'd wanted to run. Nothing would have stopped them had they gone. They could have left him there to die. But they hadn't.

The platoon was watching the planes. Grant got to his feet, unsteady and weaving. He saw something white far out in front. A moment later he knew that it would be the Tuaregs, beating a hasty retreat from a method of warfare they did not like nor understand.

Presently the planes came over the *murette* and dipped. A pilot waved his hand and then the two of them droned up and to the north, growing smaller and smaller until they were lost in the metallic sky.

Grant touched Duval's arm. "Take a squad and go up there to mop up the place. Destroy all the ammunition and take what prisoners might be left alive."

Duval saluted, *"Oui, mon sergent."* He collected his men. Schwartz came up, clicked his heels smartly.

"Empaqueter," ordered Grant. "We leave immediately through the pass."

"Oui, mon sergent," said Schwartz.

Grant took a swallow of water. He was too sick to eat. The bandage was hot against his face. He'd probably have a scar there now. Ruin his beautiful face, most likely. Well, to hell with it.

Leaning against the *murette*, his attention was drawn by a Legionnaire to a small dot out on the plains. Listening to the sounds made by ammunition exploding up the pass, Grant took a pair of field glasses and studied the dots.

If he had been sick before, he was violently ill now. That was Muller and the rest of his party. And they were heading for the pass, evidently knowing that the caravan had been overcome.

Grant turned on Schwartz. "You will leave immediately, Corporal. You are senior now. I must join my party out there."

Schwartz saluted and bawled orders. In five minutes Grant stood alone in the compound, watching the party coming toward him. The sounds of the platoon receded into silence up the mountains. Their mission was fulfilled. The Tuareg threat was over.

As an afterthought, Grant shed the sergeant's tunic and folded it under his belt. Leaning against the *murette,* he closed his eyes and saw red spots dancing beneath his lids.

That was the way Sergeant Muller found him. Sergeant Muller's beefy face was very red with anger. He laid a heavy hand on Grant's shoulder.

"Here you are," roared Muller. "You worthless pig! What was the idea—" He saw then that a bandage covered the better part of Grant's face. "Oh, you're hit."

Grant nodded, dully. From his belt, his fingers painfully clumsy, he dragged the tunic, sweat stained and soggy with blood. "Here's . . . your . . . tunic . . . Sergeant. I—"

Abruptly he fell flat on his face in the dust.

Chapter Eight

A month later, in the general hospital at Sidi, Legionnaire Larry Grant sat in the warm sunshine, looking out across the parade ground.

They had told him he'd never look the same. He didn't care. They had told him he was damned lucky to be alive. Grant had guessed he was. They had told him that he had barely escaped court-martial. Grant knew that already, more than he could tell them.

But all in all, he felt very complacent, sitting there. He wasn't thinking about Lieutenant Stephans. He had ceased to do that when he found it was possible to do so without wincing. All that was dead and gone.

Sergeant Boch passed the veranda and stopped for a moment. "Feeling better?"

"Yes, sir," said Grant with a smile.

"Carry on," replied Boch, departing.

Two officers strolled by, all gold braid and glitter. A company clerk passed them, saluting. One of the officers stopped the clerk.

"Did you find out anything?" asked the officer.

"No, sir," replied the clerk. "The platoon is in the barracks now, resting up after all that scrapping in the pass down

Ahaggar way. I asked them, sir, but none of them know how to describe the fellow except that he looked more like a gentleman than a sergeant."

"That's a hell of a description," snapped the other officer. "What did you say he did, Pierre?"

Pierre slapped his riding crop against his boot and smiled. "Saved the platoon after the lieutenant and sergeant were killed. Got word through at the risk of his life—and then vanished. Nobody seems to have known his name."

"Huh," said the other. "You mentioned something about a decoration."

"Yes, there's one waiting for him."

"I saw it this morning," volunteered the company clerk. "It's written out to Sergeant X."

Pierre slapped his boot again; the clerk saluted and moved on. The two officers wandered away through the yellow sunshine.

Grant smiled and looked at Boch far across the grounds. Boch was busy lacing down a couple of *bleus* who were out of uniform.

Red Sand

Red Sand

PERHAPS it was the desert cold; perhaps it was the predawn blackness. Whatever it was, Hardesty felt a sudden chill.

Walking to his post across the compound, unable to see a foot to either side, he had heard a soft rasp—probably some sentry changing his position. A second later the rasp was repeated and a man's hard breathing was loud and hoarse in the blackness.

All the manhunter in Legionnaire Hardesty came swimming to the surface, bursting through as a man does after long submersion. He ran swiftly toward the place he had heard it, leaped up the unseen staircase which led to the embrasures and groped in front of him.

A heavy thump sounded close beside him. He reached out with his stubby arms, grabbing at thin air. His fingers touched cloth. Abruptly he felt as though an earthquake had jarred the Moroccan mountains. A heavy fist struck him full in the face. A bayonet slithered by his throat.

To save himself he leaped backward. Space snatched him and he hurtled back to the compound. Jumping up he once more started for the steps. Although he could not see, some sixth sense guided him back to the spot which had brought the first combat.

The heavy silence of the mountains and desert, so still that it actually could be heard, was once more settling on the legion post. Hardesty, every muscle tense, waited for something to happen.

A gray line appeared in the east, turned brighter. Hardesty still waited. A shaft of sunlight struck a peak above and the world was faintly alight.

He could see Kaslov hunched over the machine gun above the wall gate. Kaslov's shoulders were tremendous things. His head was out of proportion—too small. His hands were three times the size of an ordinary man's. The Russian was nearly six feet six and as brawny as a bull.

"Kaslov," said Hardesty, his somewhat squeaky voice very tight.

Kaslov did not move and then Legionnaire Hardesty remembered. Some weeks before Kaslov had attacked a Berber stronghold with the others of the company. The Berbers had had a small one-pounder, stolen from France. Kaslov had bodily uprooted the gun, but, unfortunately, it had gone off close to his head. Kaslov was almost deaf, almost blind.

Hardesty strode forward and touched the Russian's shoulder. The man jumped and whirled about, hand on his bayonet. When he identified Hardesty, he grunted. "Oh, so it is you. You are late."

Hardesty knew he was late in his relief. But that had been caused by the scuffle on the battlement. "Did you hear anything up here, Kaslov?" asked Hardesty.

"Nothing."

"Did you see anything during your watch?"

Kaslov's small eyes were impudent as he gazed at Hardesty's sleeve. "Huh. I do not see any chevrons."

Hardesty, a foot shorter than the Russian, adjusted his kepi. He did not touch the peak. He placed his hand on one side of it as one handles a bowler hat.

"No, maybe you don't see any chevrons," said Hardesty, "but you're liable to see lots of stars. Go on to bed."

The Russian looked half minded to break Hardesty between his two hands. Then he noticed that it was light, and refrained. Grumbling, he slouched down the steps and to his barrack room.

"Now," said Hardesty, staring at the retreating back, "what in the hell ailed him? His bayonet was backward in its sheath. I wonder—"

He sat down, straddling the saddle of the machine gun. Of course, he hadn't had any right to question Kaslov. Doggone it, this instinct of his would get him into trouble yet. The High Atlas had no bearing on Chicago. And Detective-Sergeant Flaherty was a long ways back from Legionnaire Hardesty.

He fidgeted with the loading handle, looking down the narrow pass. Sometimes the Berbers got funny ideas about dawn. The lieutenant ought to be up here by this time, looking things over.

Wondering who could have attacked him so pointlessly, he shoved his kepi over his right eye and scratched his head. His face was very round. He did not tan at all; he burned raw. He certainly did not make a very impressive soldier. But then he had been trained to find men, not to kill them. Some day, he supposed, they'd tell him that politics had changed back home. When that happened, he could return. The last gang and their crooked frame had certainly been tough on his reputation.

Ah, well, he guessed he'd better forget all that. Failing to see any non-coms about, much less the lieutenant, he searched out a cigarette, jabbed it in the corner of his mouth as though it were a cigar and started to light it.

His roving eye caught sight of a sparkle on the span over the gate. He stared at it, frowning. The match burned down and singed his fingers. Without any exclamation whatever, he dropped it.

"Blood," he whispered. "For heaven's sake—"

Moving swiftly away from the machine gun he touched the red spot. It was almost solid, and when it had touched the place first it had been old.

The pale daylight showed everything in clear detail now. He thrust his head over the wall and stared down.

"A stiff!"

Unconsciously, he gnawed on the cigarette, staring at the inert body. The thing down there was horribly slashed and mangled.

Turning he saw that Corporal Bereaux had come out of the barracks. "Hey," cried Hardesty. "Hey, corporal! There's a stiff down there in front of the gate!"

Bereaux, tall and dark, a perfect martinet, ran swiftly up the steps to Hardesty's side. He stared down and his swarthy face went chalk-white.

"Damn those Berbers!" snapped Bereaux. "Go get the sergeant, quick!"

Hardesty blinked at the order and then ran across the compound toward Sergeant Schnapp's quarters. He hammered loudly on the door.

Presently, Schnapp's hard face and chill eye appeared in the crack. "What is it you want, *hein*?"

"Sergeant, there's a stiff in front of the gate," said Hardesty.

"Well, why call me, *hein*? Why not call the lieutenant?" A buckle jangled within and Sergeant Schnapp came forth, hitching his coat up over his beefy shoulders.

Schnapp did not go to the embrasures. He took down the bars and opened the gates wide. His face did not change when he saw the object. He merely grunted and knelt down.

By the grapevine operating in all military units, the men knew. They came pouring out of the squad rooms, across the bare compound, to stare over Schnapp's shoulder.

Schnapp grunted again and picked the body up.

"Wait a minute," said Hardesty, urgently. "Don't touch him!"

Schnapp glared and shouldered through. "Want to get shot by the Berbers, *hein*? What do you think they left this for, *hein*? Get inside, you pigs!"

The stiffened corpse was laid, not too tenderly, upon the bare stone. Schnapp ordered the gate closed and then stared up at the lieutenant's office.

Instantly, his eyes came back to the corpse. There was very little left of the face. The throat had been cut. The arms had been slit open and dried blood covered the uniform, obliterating its marking.

"My heavens!" cried Corporal Bereaux. "It's the lieutenant!"

"Sure it is," snapped Hardesty. "Who'd you think it was—Napoleon? Listen, *mon sergent*—"

"Shut up!" rapped Schnapp. "You know nothing about this. I know you were a detective somewhere else, but that makes you just a private here. Shut up!"

Hardesty shoved his kepi over his eye, gnawed at a tattered cigarette and shoved his hands in his pockets. His red face grew redder and his small eyes spun with anger.

"Get up on the embrasures!" ordered Schnapp. "Who told you to leave that gun, *hein*?"

Hardesty went, very sullenly. Once more he straddled the seat of the machine gun and listened to the squabble below.

"Those Berbers," growled Schnapp, "caught him when he was out on reconnoiter, yes. They took him apart like this and left him here for us to see. Those Berbers want this post, yes. If they get this post they will run their guns down here, yes. They think they can scare us out, *hein*?"

Corporal Bereaux's regulation voice came up to Hardesty. "But they can't be allowed to get away with this. We ought to tear out there and wipe them up."

"That's a good idea. Teach those pigs a lesson, *hein*? Yes, corporal, that's a good idea. Trumpeter! Sound *aux armes*. Squads one and three—"

Hardesty snorted in disgust and fumbled with the loading handle. By leaning out a little he could see the spot where the body had lain; he could see the red stains in the sand.

Looking over his shoulder, he saw the Russian, Kaslov,

shoulder stolidly past Bereaux, head down, scowling. Kaslov stared up at the embrasure, glared at Hardesty and walked on into the squad room.

Hardesty watched squads one and three depart down the pass, loaded with rifles, Chauchats, grenades. Vengeance was all right, guessed Hardesty, but it was feeble solace to his outraged professional training.

At eight o'clock he went down to eat his breakfast, turning the machine gun over to his relief. At the rough table he slapped down his pannikin and canteen cup and began to eat.

Presently a Legionnaire known as Tou-Tou, onetime sewer rat of Paris, seated himself across the board. "So the lieutenant got his, eh?"

Hardesty bobbed his head.

"I was across the fort when it happened," said Tou-Tou. "I couldn't leave my post, you see."

Hardesty looked up, frowning a little. "No, you couldn't at that, could you?"

"No, of course not. The conceit of those Berbers is pretty awful, isn't it?" said Tou-Tou. "I see by the marks on the top of the gate that they tried to lift him over the edge, leaving him right in the compound. But the lieutenant slipped back, I guess."

"Yes, guess so," replied Hardesty, eating. But his red face was unnaturally flushed and his eyes were restless.

"Funny you didn't hear it," said Tou-Tou with a knowing smile. "But then, none of us liked the lieutenant, *hein*? But it's a pity, it's a pity."

"What do you mean?" snapped Hardesty, scowling.

"Some say you get money from the United States," replied Tou-Tou, his bitter face wreathed into a greasy smile.

Hardesty very carefully picked up his pannikin. Without any warning whatever he pitched it, contents and all, into Tou-Tou's face.

The former apache yelled shrilly, leaping back. But before he could get to his knife, Hardesty launched himself across the table and grabbed him. Bodily, Hardesty pitched the squirming Tou-Tou out through the door.

Hardesty wiped his hands on his khaki pants and turned to the popeyed cook. "Get me another plate of grub," ordered Hardesty.

The cook, for the first time in legion history, complied, without a word.

At eight that night, Hardesty went on duty again. He seated himself on the machine-gun saddle, gnawing on a cold cigarette, and watched the pearly radiance of the upcoming moon.

He lifted his kepi on the side, replaced it and gave it a pat on top to drive it down. Back in Chicago, if politics were running all right, they'd be after him for his opinion. Yes, indeed, they would. The newspaper boys wouldn't have left his side for a moment. His phone would be hysterical, trying to keep up with the rings. Everything would be order.

But here. Hell, here he was nothing but a damned Legionnaire, trained bayonet unit. He wished he could get a crack at some of those big cases back home. Those were the babies. He knew every crook in Cook County. He knew every joint. Take that bank robbery he'd just read about in Sidi. He'd have solved that by now. And back home they'd still be fumbling. Too bad he'd been framed and sent away—to this.

His keen eyes picked up a moving shadow in the trail. Sitting erect he held the trips, ready for any Berbers who might spring out of nowhere.

Tensely he sat there, waiting. The shadow was taking the center of the trail. A shaft of moonlight struck the silhouette. It was grotesque, all out of shape. What in the name of Heaven was—

Suddenly he understood. Whirling, he bellowed, "Corporal of the guard! Corporal of the guard!"

The corporal came running, side arms jangling and thumping.

"Open the gate!" said Hardesty. "Two Legionnaires are coming up the trail."

The corporal unbarred the entrance. The small port swung open with a dismal creak.

Presently a man staggered through, carrying another. Hardesty, jumpy with excitement, started to leave the gun and then remembered that, after all, he was a soldier now, not a manhunter.

Corporal Bereaux eased the Russian, Kaslov, to the pavement and stood there, spent and panting, while the corporal of the guard slammed shut the gates.

"What happened?" demanded the corporal of the guard.

Bereaux sank down and mopped at his forehead. "I don't know what happened!"

Kaslov moaned and rolled a little.

"What's the matter with him?" demanded the corporal of the guard.

"Slugged," stated Bereaux. "I had . . . had to carry him for three miles. Lord, but he's heavy."

"Where are the others?" demanded the corporal of the guard.

Bereaux moaned, "They're dead—all of them. I . . . I was sent out to reconnoiter. I heard firing behind me and tried to get back, but I fell down a ravine and when I could get to them— Lord, but it was horrible! They were dead! Ambush!"

Kaslov sat up unsteadily. Legionnaires had poured out of the barracks, surrounding the two.

"He was the only one left alive. He was far behind the others, working a Chauchat." Bereaux stopped, breathing heavily.

"Didn't you see it?" demanded the corporal of the guard to Kaslov.

"No. One burst of fire, my eardrums close. I can hear nothing. I got hit with something on the head, but . . . but I see no blood." Kaslov felt gingerly of his skull.

Bereaux stood up, angrily, the perfect non-com. "Why you filthy louse! You ugly hog! You made me carry you for miles because you said you couldn't walk."

A chuckle ran about the circle and was then instantly still. It had suddenly occurred to them that they numbered eighteen and that they were completely without command. The lieutenant was gone. Sergeant Schnapp had gone along with two of the squads, three and one.

A platoon at first, they were now but half a platoon. True,

they had three corporals. The corporal of the guard realized what they faced. He turned to Bereaux.

"You're senior," said the corporal of the guard.

Bereaux, rocking on his feet with weariness, blinked about him. "Eighteen men? But by Heaven, the Berbers want this post! They'll—" He checked himself but the rest understood.

Hardesty nodded slowly, shifted his kepi, looking down from his post at the gun.

"Someone will have to reconnoiter," stated Bereaux. "We can't afford to be surprised. Neither can we afford to fill all the posts all the time."

"I'll go," said Hardesty, rather surprised at the loudness of his voice. He realized then that he was under a strain.

Bereaux stared up, swarthy face very tired in the moonlight. "Ah, the detective. Well, go then."

Hardesty surrendered his post to another Legionnaire and climbed down to the compound. He procured his rifle and a canteen of water.

"Where," said Hardesty, "did the Berbers ambush the squads?"

Bereaux shook his head. "Not out there. Just scout the front and get back."

Kaslov's brute face turned away. "If he can," muttered Kaslov.

Hardesty went through the gate. He could hear the murmur behind him. He could hear Tou-Tou's wail, "We'll be slaughtered!"

Hardesty's hobnails rasped and scraped on the stones in the pass. The moon cast his shadow behind him, conjured up other shadows to the fore. But Hardesty did not try to go either quietly or cautiously.

He could trace the tracks in the sand. Seventeen men leave ample evidence of their passage, even by moonlight. At the end of a half-hour he found himself trotting across a smooth plain which ended in a ravine—a black gash across the silver of the world.

He was thinking furiously. So the Berbers wanted this post, did they? Just how bad did they need it? So they could run their guns down this pass, Schnapp had said. Perhaps Schnapp was right. That had been foolish of Schnapp—going out that way. He had no business deserting his command.

Fifteen minutes later Hardesty was beside the ravine. There was ample cover here—boulders, holes, niches along the cliff walls.

Down below huddled a group of shadows, almost in formation. Hardesty stopped, adjusting his kepi again. He tramped down the slope of the hill and stopped again.

Schnapp's head had been blown away. He had been following the squads. The next row of men were hacked through the shoulders. The next had gotten it in the chest. And the front rank had been smashed through the small of their backs.

Hardesty grunted. They were all dead in their tracks—killed almost instantly. Hadn't they covered themselves any better than that? Oh, yes, with Kaslov and an auto-rifle.

Hardesty sighted back up the slope. He knew the exact angle of fire because of the bullets in the targets. It was a rather gruesome calculation, but Hardesty knew that the gun which had mowed them down had been high and to the rear.

He backtracked swiftly. Suddenly he saw the scattered empties which had spewed out of the breach. They were all in one square yard. The gunner had not moved. The guns were gone, of course. Leave that to the Berbers.

Picking up a couple of the brass shells, Hardesty headed for home. There was nothing he could do here—not now. Perhaps they'd send out a burial party. Perhaps they would bring the men into the fort. That was not his worry.

Shadows were jumpy ahead of him. He knew what a fine target he made out here in the moonlight. If the Berbers were about, they'd make short work of him.

Hardesty slogged back to the pass. Three miles were not much, even for him. He slowed down when he came to the incline. Far ahead he could see the corner of the fort, guarding this one and only pass across these barren peaks.

A hundred yards from the corner, Hardesty stopped. In the next few steps he would come into sight of the gate. Better test the gunner up there. No telling what might happen.

Hardesty took a boulder the size of his head and heaved it. It crashed into the trail and rolled. Instantly a machine gun chattered. Slugs yowled and spanged away from the rock walls.

Mopping his brow, Hardesty sat down. That had been very close—entirely too close. When the gun stopped, he stood up, cupping his hands and yelled, "Hey! It's Hardesty! Hold that fire!"

An answer drifted back to him, very thin and far, "Come ahead!"

Taking the shadowy side of the wall, Hardesty went toward the gate. He expected to be plugged any instant, either by the machine gun up there or possible Berbers. He held his breath and paused every few steps. But no sound came out of the fort, nor from the pass.

He reached the gate and rapped upon it. In a second it swung back, disclosing the face of Tou-Tou. "Oh," he said, "you got back, I see. Any Berbers?"

Hardesty shouldered past the man and then stopped. The two squads were drawn up in heavy marching order in the center of the parade ground.

Amazed, Hardesty ambled toward them. Bereaux turned and watched him come.

"But," said Hardesty, "you're not thinking of deserting this post, are you?"

Bitterness was in Bereaux's voice. "I'm not thinking about it, but these fools will have it no other way. They see themselves torn to pieces by Berber knives."

Tou-Tou took his place in the ranks, grinning. Up on the embrasure, Kaslov stared down.

"Did he shoot at me?" demanded Hardesty, pointing to the Russian.

Kaslov swung down, leaving his post. "Yes, I shot at you. I get orders to hold the pass, I shot thinking I saw Berbers." He was scowling.

"Get back up there!" snapped Bereaux.

"I'm not covering a retreat," growled Kaslov. "I don't get left behind again."

Hardesty squared off, facing the Russian. "Did you fire any rounds today from your Chauchat rifles?"

Taken a little by surprise, the Russian shook his head. "No."

"You're lying," snapped Hardesty.

Kaslov advanced, arms swinging at his sides. "Are you big enough to say that I lie?"

Bereaux drew out a pistol he had found in the lieutenant's quarters. "Back, Kaslov. What's the matter, Hardesty?"

"There was a mound of empties up there where the two squads got it." He reached into his pocket and pulled out the shells. "See that bright streak along the side? These were shot out of an auto-rifle, French. A legion gun killed those men!"

The ranks shifted. Men drifted forward.

Kaslov stared at the empty. "You . . . you think I did that, eh? You think I shot my own men, eh? You lie!" He lifted his hands and started to grab Hardesty.

Hardesty deliberately turned to Bereaux. "When you picked him up, had the Chauchat been fired?"

"Yes," replied Bereaux. "I remember seeing the empties now that I think of it. I naturally thought the murderer was trying to help out the squads."

Hardesty turned to Kaslov. The Russian was staring about him at the menacing faces of the other Legionnaires.

Hardesty smiled, but not humorously. He was having his day, now. They were paying some attention to him at last. They would monkey with murder, would they?

"Tou-Tou," said Hardesty, "empty a cartridge case right here on the parade ground."

Tou-Tou glanced about him and then brought the ammunition. The shells spilled out in a heap, brilliant in the moonlight.

"What are you going to do?" snarled Kaslov.

Hardesty picked up a handful of the shells. "Lay down, Kaslov. Flat on your face."

Kaslov growled, "To hell with you."

Hardesty reached out, grasped the Russian's wrist and suddenly Kaslov was flat on his face.

"Jujitsu," said Hardesty, complacently. "Now, you Legionnaires, crowd up close here a minute. If Kaslov doesn't lay still, pin him down with your bayonets."

Scooping up cartridges, Hardesty started flipping them across the Russian, exactly as though the shells were streaming out of the smoking breech of a Chauchat.

Mystified, anger and punishment held in check only by curiosity, the Legionnaires looked on. They saw Kaslov's mammoth shoulders become surrounded by the brass cases.

Hardesty stood up, watchfully. He grabbed Kaslov's collar and jerked Kaslov to his feet. The Russian, realizing that a move for vengeance or freedom would do him no good whatever, planted his big feet sullenly on the ground and watched.

Hardesty pointed down. The Legionnaires frowned. All they saw was that the shells had left a clear space where the Russian had lain. In fact, they could see the tremendous shape of his shoulders and arms.

"That's the pattern of the empties out there," stated Hardesty. "If any of you want, you can go out and look for yourself.

*Hardesty reached out, grasped the Russian's wrist and
suddenly Kaslov was flat on his face.*

In other words, Kaslov was lying down when the Chauchat gun was fired!"

And before any of them could grasp that fact, Hardesty whirled on the corporal. "Bereaux! You're the man!

"You killed the lieutenant, Bereaux! You sent me for the sergeant when you should have sent me for the lieutenant. Although no one could recognize that corpse outside the gate, you knew the lieutenant was dead!

"You slaughtered that party! You slugged Kaslov and then brought him back to hang for you in case anybody suspected the trick! You've sold out to the Berbers! They're paying you to leave this post deserted!"

For an instant, Bereaux was stunned by the flow of words. Then he lost all semblance of his military self. He leaped forward, shouting, "You lying fool, I'll tear you apart!"

Bereaux, unused to a revolver, lifted the gun high, ready to deal a blow. Before he could bring it down he remembered the other Legionnaires and whirled obliquely. Taken by surprise, the others had not moved.

Bereaux, once more in complete control of himself, backed away to a safe distance, gun very steady. He smiled rather gruesomely. "Yes, I sold you out. What of it? Who are you, anyway? Rabble, nothing but rabble. I was once an officer!"

He was backing slowly toward the gate, revolver swinging in a steady arc. A small corporal's whistle dangled from his lanyard. He took it in his left hand. "The Berbers are waiting for you outside. The moon is at its zenith, the appointed time has come.

"I was to have led you into their fire, but failing that, I

have another plan. I go outside, seek protection and when I blow this whistle, you'll be wiped out, to a man, by the attack. You are too few to stand against the tribes—too few to stand between me and my plans."

His flare for the dramatic was manifest in his bow. He swung back the gate and stepped into the black patch of shadow outside it, leaving the portals wide open.

Hardesty glanced swiftly about him. Something glinted from another corporal's neck. Another whistle! Their lives hung on split-second threads.

With energy he had not known he had possessed, Hardesty leaped for the second whistle, placing it between his lips. Its shrill blast echoed far through the pass.

Hardesty found himself running. He heard the chattering roar of a machine gun outside. He heard the triumphant yell of a hundred men. He heard the snapping yowl of bullets.

"Man the walls!" cried Hardesty.

Throwing himself upon the gate he swung it shut. The machine gun had stopped. Sandals were sprinting up the incline. Bodies threw themselves against the opposite side of the panel.

Hardesty struggled to hold the gate. It gave slowly in. Another instant and he would be trampled under sprinting feet. Another instant and the fort would be taken. Another instant and the seventeen within the walls would be slaughtered to a man.

Straining, every tendon in his small compact body as taut as a banjo string, beads of sweat standing out against his red forehead, he strove to hold.

Above him the legion machine gun cut loose. But that would do no good if the gate were not held. Another inch inward. Another and another. Seconds were ages. His whole body ached. Curses rang loudly on the other side.

Abruptly the pressure slackened, or at least it seemed to. And then Hardesty was aware of a raging bulk beside him. The mighty-bodied Kaslov. Boards creaked in the doors. Shots splintered through. Kaslov swore in a loud bellow, holding the gate with his shoulders.

Suddenly the thing was closed. Hardesty snatched at the bars and pulled them across. A moment later, he sagged back, glowing with the knowledge that he had won.

The machine gun roared above them. Death smashed into the pass. A Chauchat started up with its hysterical clatter. They were clearing the pass with enfilade fire. Grenades exploded down on the incline, setting the night on fire with their blinding flashes.

Abruptly everything was still. A murmur started along the embrasure. The murmur grew and became a shout. Kaslov looked at Hardesty and said, "You got a cigarette?"

Hardesty handed one over and lighted it for the Russian. Kaslov dragged thankfully at it and then dug in his tunic for a flat bottle. The warmth of the fluid slid easily down Hardesty's throat.

After Kaslov had taken a drink, he wiped his lips with the back of his hand and said, "About those empties. Was that right? Did they leave a pattern around me?"

Hardesty laughed. "It was a good story, wasn't it?"

Abruptly the pressure slackened, or at least it seemed to.
And then Hardesty was aware of a raging bulk beside him.

Kaslov chuckled, then sobered. "Too bad he got away, wasn't it?"

"Wasn't it?" said Hardesty. He swung back the small inner door and pointed out. Kaslov looked through and grunted.

Riddled by the first burst, and sprawled in death amid the tribesmen, lay Corporal Bereaux, victim of ideas. Even in the pale moonlight they could see that the sand beneath the body was turning red.

Story Preview

Story Preview

NOW that you've just ventured through some of the captivating tales in the Stories from the Golden Age collection by L. Ron Hubbard, turn the page and enjoy a preview of *The Iron Duke*. Join Blacky Lee, a man wanted by nearly every government in Europe, who happens to be the spitting image of a leader in the Balkan kingdom of Aldoria. With nowhere else to hide, the enterprising Lee flees to Aldoria and attempts to make the most of his mistaken identity in a startling tale of intrigue, humor and romance.

The Iron Duke

STUB always had an uneasy feeling about Blacky Lee. Stub's state of mind was that of a man watching another holding a cannon cracker and not knowing just when he'd let that cracker explode. At least once a day Stub wondered why he had ever allowed himself to become associated with as nerve-racking a fellow as Blacky Lee. One never knew what was going on in Lee's mind and never, never knew just when those thoughts would amalgamate with a bang. And sitting there watching Blacky just now, Stub forgot all about how grateful he was for the warmth in the radiator.

Blacky Lee had come out of his reverie and was now, by aid of his reflection in the glass, carefully twirling his ginger mustache into a pair of military points. Stub, who always ran on the assumption that now, at last, he knew everything about Blacky Lee, was sorely jolted by the little container of mustache wax which Blacky was using. Never in all the years he had been with Blacky had Stub known him to carry wax or use wax, and now, with their baggage abandoned in Austria, a thing as nonsensical as mustache wax was here in Blacky's possession! Certainly Blacky was attempting no disguise, for pointing a mustache would be a very weak attempt in that direction.

Stub gave over wondering. He sighed and rested his little

round face in his pudgy hands. "There was such a *nice* bottle of anisette in my trunk," he sighed. "Do you suppose I'll ever see that bottle again, Blacky?"

"Probably never."

"And that nice new suit with the yellow stripes—"

"It's probably adorning the porter of the King's Hotel—if his taste in clothes is as bad as yours."

"Gosh! You really think so, Blacky?"

"You're lucky," said Lee, "not to have that suit full of holes—with you in back of each hole."

"Yeah. Yeah, you're always telling me how lucky I am to be alive," sighed Stub. "You pull me through hell and high dives with one of your ideas, and then when we escape on the razor edge of execution you tell me how lucky I am! I'm not complaining, you understand, but sometimes I think my nerves just won't stand it anymore. Tonight we should have been dining with generals and getting paid real money, but here we are, on a train without tickets, in a country which we didn't enter legally, without so much as an Aldorian dime or a forged birth certificate!"

"You haven't forgotten how to use a pen," said Lee.

"Yeah, but now I haven't even *got* a pen. Sometimes, Blacky—"

The train came to a screaming halt, nearly throwing Stub into the middle of the floor. He clutched the sill, staring with terrified eyes at Blacky.

"That conductor saw us. The Austrians figured we'd shuttle across the frontier and snag this rattler! Hell's bells, Blacky, what are we going to do now?"

"Sit tight and hope," said Blacky Lee imperturbably. "It's impossible that they could have extradited us that fast."

"They'd send word that we were in the country without papers," groaned Stub. "Blacky, I can hear the rats in the dungeons already!"

Blacky was giving the troops outside the window an interested examination. A patrol, booted and greatcoated, was splashing flashlights along the side of the track and boarding the train at the next car.

"We're in for it now," said Stub. "And me without so much as a drink!"

Stub twisted his neck so that he could look up the track at the somber figures of the patrol, and then, when he next glanced at Blacky Lee and saw that a 9 mm Webley showed its snout from beneath Blacky's folded topcoat, his eyes got big and then narrow. Stub, without sigh or protest, put his hand into his side pocket and gripped the butt of the Colt Police Positive .38 therein. If Blacky was going to make a fight for it even against a large and well-armed patrol, then it would be a fight.

They sat very still, though there was no perceptible change in Blacky, hearing the patrol going through the cars ahead, hearing the complaints of roused passengers who, having had to stay up to pass through the frontier, now thought they were being slightly imposed upon. The search was coming closer, compartment by compartment.

Their compartment door was thrown open by the trainmaster, who consulted his record so as to address the occupants by name and save them as much embarrassment as he could. The trainmaster's watery eyes came up with a jerk from the record and drilled Blacky Lee.

The lieutenant in charge of the patrol was all business. He had stripped off his great gauntlets and tucked them in his belt, but he had his crop in hand and was cutting nervously at his boots as he waited for the trainmaster to speak up.

"Well?" said the dark-faced lieutenant.

"Your honor," said the trainmaster, trembling, "I have no record of the two gentlemen in there."

"Ah!" And the lieutenant, with all the savor of a bloodhound at last treeing his quarry, thrust himself into the room, one hand resting on the butt of his gun.

Stub was waiting for the shot that would start the war. He could see the troopers in the corridor and the dull gleam of their carbines, and he knew how slight were his chances. But he had an accurate bead upon the lieutenant's greatcoat, third button from the top.

The lieutenant's smile of triumph suddenly congealed upon his face and then, from the eyes down, there dropped a curtain of fumbling terror. This, in turn, was swept away by a stolid parade-ground expression and looking straight ahead, his heels close together, the lieutenant spoke.

"My apologies, Your Highness. We are searching for one Balchard, leader of the Sons of Freedom, reported to have been on this train. My stupidity, Your Highness, is only that of zeal. May I be granted the favor of remaining aboard and posting adequate guard over your compartment?"

"I do not care," said Blacky Lee, "to have attention called

to my presence aboard the Trans-Balkan Express. You are excused, Lieutenant. Carry on."

The lieutenant, embarrassed, about-faced and marched out. Angrily he motioned his men from the corridor.

The trainmaster stood blinking and peering, stupefied, and undoubtedly promising himself a new set of glasses, pride or no pride, at the next stopover.

"Is . . . is there anything Your Highness could wish, sire?"

"Yes," said Blacky Lee. "A bottle of anisette for my friend and a ham sandwich for myself."

"Immediately, Your Highness." And he stumbled away.

Stub looked, slack-jawed, at Blacky Lee, finding it difficult to force a question out of his constricted throat.

"Your Highness?" gulped Stub. "He—they called you 'Your Highness'!"

Blacky Lee smiled enigmatically and slid the Webley 9 mm into his side pocket. The train had started again and he sank back, staring thoughtfully out of the window at the flying night. . . .

To find out more about *The Iron Duke* and how you can obtain your copy, go to www.goldenagestories.com.

Glossary

STORIES FROM THE GOLDEN AGE *reflect the words and expressions used in the 1930s and 1940s, adding unique flavor and authenticity to the tales. While a character's speech may often reflect regional origins, it also can convey attitudes common in the day. So that readers can better grasp such cultural and historical terms, uncommon words or expressions of the era, the following glossary has been provided.*

Ahaggar Plateau: a highland region in the central Sahara, located in southern Algeria. It is an arid, rocky upland region and the home of the formerly nomadic Tuareg.

apache: a Parisian gangster or thug. The term was first used in 1902 by a French journalist to describe Paris thieves who were known for their crimes of violence. Apaches were so called because their alleged savagery was compared with that attributed by Europeans to the Native American tribes of Apaches.

aux armes: (French) to arms.

bandolier: a broad belt worn over the shoulder by soldiers and having a number of small loops or pockets for holding cartridges.

"Bang Away, Lulu": a Navy/Marine song about a woman named Lulu.

barker: someone who stands in front of a show at a carnival and gives a loud colorful sales talk to potential customers.

bataillon pénal: (French) penal battalion; military unit consisting of convicted persons for whom military service was either assigned punishment or a voluntary replacement of imprisonment. Penal battalion service was very dangerous: the official view was that they were highly expendable and were to be used to reduce losses in regular units. Convicts were released from their term of service early if they suffered a combat injury (the crime was considered to be "washed out with blood") or performed a heroic deed.

Berbers: members of a people living in North Africa, primarily Muslim, living in settled or nomadic tribes between the Sahara and Mediterranean Sea and between Egypt and the Atlantic Ocean.

bleus: (French) raw recruits; newcomers.

boot: 1. saddle boot; a close-fitting covering or case for a gun or other weapon that straps to a saddle. **2.** a Marine recruit in basic training.

bowler: derby; a hard felt hat with a rounded crown and narrow brim, created by James Lock & Co, a firm founded in 1676 in London. The prototype was made in 1850 for a customer of Lock's by Thomas and William Bowler, hat makers in Southwark, England. At first it was dubbed the *iron hat* because it was hard enough to protect the head, and later picked up the name *bowler* because of its makers' family name. In the US it became known as a *derby* from its association with the Kentucky Derby.

campaigner: campaign hat; a felt hat with a broad stiff brim and four dents in the crown, formerly worn by personnel in the US Army and Marine Corps.

cannon cracker: a large firecracker.

carbines: short light rifles, originally used by soldiers on horses.

Chauchat: a light machine gun used mainly by the French Army. It was among the first light machine-gun designs of the early 1900s. It set a precedent for twentieth-century firearm projects as it could be built inexpensively in very large numbers.

Colt Police Positive .38: a .38-caliber revolver developed by the Colt Firearms Company in answer to a demand for a more powerful version of the .32-caliber Police Positive. First introduced in 1905, these guns were sold to many US police forces and European military units, as well as being made available to the general public.

cork off: go to bed; sleep.

corpsman: an enlisted member of the Navy Medical Corps trained in field medical aid, especially in combat situations. They usually wear Marine Corps uniforms with Navy rank and insignia.

cur: a mean, cowardly person.

"cut of the vest": execution where the victim's head was cut with a machete, the arms were then severed at the shoulders and a design etched on the chest with machete slashes.

deck court: the lowest of naval courts. It is a court composed of one commissioned officer for the trial of enlisted men for minor offenses. The deck court cannot adjudge a punishment greater than twenty days' confinement or twenty days' solitary confinement, and twenty days' loss of pay.

¿De donde viene el caballo?: (Spanish) Where is the horse from?

dixies: mess tins or oval pots often used in camp for cooking or boiling.

¿Donde estás?: (Spanish) Where are you?

drome: short for airdrome; a military air base.

empaqueter: (French) pack up.

G-men: government men; agents of the Federal Bureau of Investigation.

gob: a sailor in the US Navy.

goldbrick: a person, especially a soldier, who avoids assigned duties or work.

grandstand play: a showy action or move, as in a sport, in order to gain attention or approval.

grifter: crooked game operator; a person who operates a sideshow at a circus, fair, etc., especially a gambling attraction.

Guardia: Nicaraguan National Guard; *Guardia Nacional.* This militia was formed in Nicaragua during US occupation in 1925. A long period of civil strife had encouraged the development of a variety of private armies. The freshly elected government requested that the US Marines (equally interested in central control) remain in Nicaragua until an indigenous security force could be trained. The Nicaraguan government hired a retired US general to establish the *Guardia Nacional de Nicaragua*. US forces left in 1925, but after a brief resurgence of violence, returned in 1926, taking over command of the *Guardia Nacional* until 1933, when it was returned to Nicaraguan control under the government.

gyrene: a Marine.

HE: high explosive.

hein?: (French) eh?

heliograph: a device for signaling by means of a movable mirror that reflects beams of light, especially sunlight, to a distance.

High Atlas: portion of the Atlas Mountain range that rises in the west at the Atlantic coast and stretches in an eastern direction to the Moroccan-Algerian border.

hobnail: a short nail with a thick head used to increase the durability of a boot sole.

Irish pennants: loose threads hanging from a Naval or Marine uniform, considered untidy.

joyeux: (French) from *Les Joyeux,* "the joyful." The common name for a member of the penal battalions because they were always complaining.

jujitsu: an art of weaponless self-defense developed in Japan that uses throws, holds and blows. It derives added power from the attacker's own weight and strength.

kepi: a cap with a circular top and a nearly horizontal visor; a French military cap that men in the Foreign Legion wear.

leatherneck: a member of the US Marine Corps. The phrase comes from the early days of the Marine Corps when enlisted men were given strips of leather to wear around their necks. The popular concept was that the leather protected the neck from a saber slash, though it was actually used to keep the Marines from slouching in uniform by forcing them to keep their heads up.

Legionnaire: a member of the French Foreign Legion, a unique elite unit within the French Army established in 1831. It was created as a unit for foreign volunteers and was primarily used to protect and expand the French colonial empire during the nineteenth century, but has also taken part in all of France's wars with other European powers. It is known to be an elite military unit whose training focuses not only on traditional military skills, but also on the building of a strong *esprit de corps* amongst members. As its men come from different countries with different cultures, this is a widely accepted solution to strengthen them enough to work as a team. Training is often not only physically hard with brutal training methods, but also extremely stressful with high rates of desertion.

martinet: a rigid military disciplinarian.

midway: an avenue or area at a carnival where the concessions for exhibitions of curiosities, games of chance, scenes from foreign life, merry-go-rounds, and other rides and amusements are located.

¡Mira! ¡Mira! ¡Yanquis!: (Spanish) Look! Look! Yankees!

mon brave: (French) my brave one; my courageous one.

mon sergent: (French) my sergeant.

Moroccan mountains: Moroccan Atlas ranges; a portion of the Atlas Mountain range lying completely in Morocco.

mountain rifle: a very long, ruggedly built rifle designed for use in mountainous terrain.

mulligan: mulligan stew; a stew made from whatever ingredients are available.

murette: (French) a low wall.

musette bag: a general-purpose canvas bag with a shoulder strap used by soldiers.

one-pounder: a gun firing a one-pound shot or shell. It looks somewhat like a miniature cannon.

¡Oye! ¿Que pasa?: (Spanish) Hey! What's happening?

¡Oye, Ramón! ¿Donde estás?: (Spanish) Hey, Ramón! Where are you?

panels: ground-to-air panel system; a system used by ground troops to communicate, to a limited degree, with aircraft by displaying black and white panels on the ground to transmit brief messages or to identify a unit.

pannikin: a small pan, often of tin.

PC: Post Command; military installation where the command personnel are located.

pipe down: turn in; release from duties and go to bed.

puttee: a covering for the lower part of the leg from the ankle to the knee, consisting of a long narrow piece of cloth wound tightly and spirally round the leg, and serving both as a support and protection. It was once adopted as part of the uniform of foot and mounted soldiers in several armies.

¿Que pasó?: (Spanish) What happened?

¿Quién sabe?: (Spanish) Who knows?

Quoi?: (French) What?

rattler: a fast freight train.

salopard: (French) an offensive expression for a detestable person.

Scheherazade: the female narrator of *The Arabian Nights,* who during one thousand and one adventurous nights saved her life by entertaining her husband, the king, with stories.

shavetail: a second lieutenant.

Sidi: Sidi-bel-Abbès, which is a capital of the Sidi-bel-Abbès province in northwestern Algeria. The city was developed around a French camp built in 1843. From 1931 until 1961, the city was the "holy city" or spiritual home of the French Foreign Legion, the location of its basic training camp and the headquarters of its first foreign regiment.

solo: (Spanish) alone.

Springfield: any of several types of rifle, named after Springfield, Massachusetts, the site of a federal armory that made the rifles.

top kick: a first sergeant, the senior enlisted grade authorized in a company.

Tuaregs: members of the nomadic Berber-speaking people of the southwestern Sahara in Africa. They have traditionally engaged in herding, agriculture and convoying caravans across their territories. The Tuaregs became among the most hostile of all the colonized peoples of French West Africa, because they were among the most affected by colonial policies. In 1917, they fought a vicious and bloody war against the French, but they were defeated and as a result, dispossessed of traditional grazing lands. They are known to be fierce warriors; European explorers expressed their fear by warning, "The scorpion and the Tuareg are the only enemies you meet in the desert."

twenty-two or **.22 rifle:** .22-caliber rifle. The relatively short effective range, low report and light recoil have made it a favorite for use in target practice. With its quiet report, it is ideal for indoor shooting or in areas that are confined.

two bits: a quarter; during the colonial days, people used coins from all over the world. When the US adopted an official currency, the Spanish milled (machine-struck) dollar was chosen and it later became the model for American silver dollars. Milled dollars were easily cut apart into equal "bits" of eight pieces. Two bits would equal a quarter of a dollar.

USMC: United States Marine Corps.

volley fire: simultaneous artillery fire in which each piece is fired a specified number of rounds without regard to the other pieces, and as fast as accuracy will permit.

Webley: Webley and Scott handgun; an arms manufacturer based in England that produced handguns from 1834. Webley is famous for the revolvers and automatic pistols it supplied to the British Empire's military, particularly the British Army, from 1887 through both World War I and World War II.

yanqui: (Spanish) Yankee; term used to refer to Americans in general.

L. Ron Hubbard
in the Golden Age
of Pulp Fiction

*In writing an adventure story
a writer has to know that he is adventuring
for a lot of people who cannot.
The writer has to take them here and there
about the globe and show them
excitement and love and realism.
As long as that writer is living the part of an
adventurer when he is hammering
the keys, he is succeeding with his story.*

*Adventuring is a state of mind.
If you adventure through life, you have a
good chance to be a success on paper.*

*Adventure doesn't mean globe-trotting,
exactly, and it doesn't mean great deeds.
Adventuring is like art.
You have to live it to make it real.*

—*L. RON HUBBARD*

L. Ron Hubbard
and American
Pulp Fiction

ORN March 13, 1911, L. Ron Hubbard lived a life at least as expansive as the stories with which he enthralled a hundred million readers through a fifty-year career.

Originally hailing from Tilden, Nebraska, he spent his formative years in a classically rugged Montana, replete with the cowpunchers, lawmen and desperadoes who would later people his Wild West adventures. And lest anyone imagine those adventures were drawn from vicarious experience, he was not only breaking broncs at a tender age, he was also among the few whites ever admitted into Blackfoot society as a bona fide blood brother. While if only to round out an otherwise rough and tumble youth, his mother was that rarity of her time—a thoroughly educated woman—who introduced her son to the classics of Occidental literature even before his seventh birthday.

But as any dedicated L. Ron Hubbard reader will attest, his world extended far beyond Montana. In point of fact, and as the son of a United States naval officer, by the age of eighteen he had traveled over a quarter of a million miles. Included therein were three Pacific crossings to a then still mysterious Asia, where he ran with the likes of Her British Majesty's agent-in-place

L. Ron Hubbard, left, at Congressional Airport, Washington, DC, 1931, with members of George Washington University flying club.

for North China, and the last in the line of Royal Magicians from the court of Kublai Khan. For the record, L. Ron Hubbard was also among the first Westerners to gain admittance to forbidden Tibetan monasteries below Manchuria, and his photographs of China's Great Wall long graced American geography texts.

Upon his return to the United States and a hasty completion of his interrupted high school education, the young Ron Hubbard entered George Washington University. There, as fans of his aerial adventures may have heard, he earned his wings as a pioneering barnstormer at the dawn of American aviation. He also earned a place in free-flight record books for the longest sustained flight above Chicago. Moreover, as a roving reporter for *Sportsman Pilot* (featuring his first professionally penned articles), he further helped inspire a generation of pilots who would take America to world airpower.

Immediately beyond his sophomore year, Ron embarked on the first of his famed ethnological expeditions, initially to then untrammeled Caribbean shores (descriptions of which would later fill a whole series of West Indies mystery-thrillers). That the Puerto Rican interior would also figure into the future of Ron Hubbard stories was likewise no accident. For in addition to cultural studies of the island, a 1932–33

LRH expedition is rightly remembered as conducting the first complete mineralogical survey of a Puerto Rico under United States jurisdiction.

There was many another adventure along this vein: As a lifetime member of the famed Explorers Club, L. Ron Hubbard charted North Pacific waters with the first shipboard radio direction finder, and so pioneered a long-range navigation system universally employed until the late twentieth century. While not to put too fine an edge on it, he also held a rare Master Mariner's license to pilot any vessel, of any tonnage in any ocean.

Yet lest we stray too far afield, there is an LRH note at this juncture in his saga, and it reads in part:

"I started out writing for the pulps, writing the best I knew, writing for every mag on the stands, slanting as well as I could."

To which one might add: His earliest submissions date from the summer of 1934, and included tales drawn from true-to-life Asian adventures, with characters roughly modeled on British/American intelligence operatives he had known in Shanghai. His early Westerns were similarly peppered with details drawn from personal experience. Although therein lay a first hard lesson from the often cruel world of the pulps. His first Westerns were soundly rejected as lacking the authenticity of a Max Brand yarn

Capt. L. Ron Hubbard in Ketchikan, Alaska, 1940, on his Alaskan Radio Experimental Expedition, the first of three voyages conducted under the Explorers Club flag.

(a particularly frustrating comment given L. Ron Hubbard's Westerns came straight from his Montana homeland, while Max Brand was a mediocre New York poet named Frederick Schiller Faust, who turned out implausible six-shooter tales from the terrace of an Italian villa).

Nevertheless, and needless to say, L. Ron Hubbard persevered and soon earned a reputation as among the most publishable names in pulp fiction, with a ninety percent placement rate of first-draft manuscripts. He was also among the most prolific, averaging between seventy and a hundred thousand words a month. Hence the rumors that L. Ron Hubbard had redesigned a typewriter for faster keyboard action and pounded out manuscripts on a continuous roll of butcher paper to save the precious seconds it took to insert a single sheet of paper into manual typewriters of the day.

That all L. Ron Hubbard stories did not run beneath said byline is yet another aspect of pulp fiction lore. That is, as publishers periodically rejected manuscripts from top-drawer authors if only to avoid paying top dollar, L. Ron Hubbard and company just as frequently replied with submissions under various pseudonyms. In Ron's case, the list

---

A MAN OF MANY NAMES

Between 1934 and 1950, L. Ron Hubbard authored more than fifteen million words of fiction in more than two hundred classic publications. To supply his fans and editors with stories across an array of genres and pulp titles, he adopted fifteen pseudonyms in addition to his already renowned L. Ron Hubbard byline.

Winchester Remington Colt
Lt. Jonathan Daly
Capt. Charles Gordon
Capt. L. Ron Hubbard
Bernard Hubbel
Michael Keith
Rene Lafayette
Legionnaire 148
Legionnaire 14830
Ken Martin
Scott Morgan
Lt. Scott Morgan
Kurt von Rachen
Barry Randolph
Capt. Humbert Reynolds

---

included: Rene Lafayette, Captain Charles Gordon, Lt. Scott Morgan and the notorious Kurt von Rachen—supposedly on the lam for a murder rap, while hammering out two-fisted prose in Argentina. The point: While L. Ron Hubbard as Ken Martin spun stories of Southeast Asian intrigue, LRH as Barry Randolph authored tales of

L. Ron Hubbard, circa 1930, at the outset of a literary career that would finally span half a century.

romance on the Western range—which, stretching between a dozen genres is how he came to stand among the two hundred elite authors providing close to a million tales through the glory days of American Pulp Fiction.

In evidence of exactly that, by 1936 L. Ron Hubbard was literally leading pulp fiction's elite as president of New York's American Fiction Guild. Members included a veritable pulp hall of fame: Lester "Doc Savage" Dent, Walter "The Shadow" Gibson, and the legendary Dashiell Hammett—to cite but a few.

Also in evidence of just where L. Ron Hubbard stood within his first two years on the American pulp circuit: By the spring of 1937, he was ensconced in Hollywood, adopting a Caribbean thriller for Columbia Pictures, remembered today as *The Secret of Treasure Island.* Comprising fifteen thirty-minute episodes, the L. Ron Hubbard screenplay led to the most profitable matinée serial in Hollywood history. In accord with Hollywood culture, he was thereafter continually called

The 1937 Secret of Treasure Island, *a fifteen-episode serial adapted for the screen by L. Ron Hubbard from his novel,* Murder at Pirate Castle.

upon to rewrite/doctor scripts—most famously for long-time friend and fellow adventurer Clark Gable.

In the interim—and herein lies another distinctive chapter of the L. Ron Hubbard story—he continually worked to open Pulp Kingdom gates to up-and-coming authors. Or, for that matter, anyone who wished to write. It was a fairly unconventional stance, as markets were already thin and competition razor sharp. But the fact remains, it was an L. Ron Hubbard hallmark that he vehemently lobbied on behalf of young authors—regularly supplying instructional articles to trade journals, guest-lecturing to short story classes at George Washington University and Harvard, and even founding his own creative writing competition. It was established in 1940, dubbed the Golden Pen, and guaranteed winners both New York representation and publication in *Argosy*.

But it was John W. Campbell Jr.'s *Astounding Science Fiction* that finally proved the most memorable LRH vehicle. While every fan of L. Ron Hubbard's galactic epics undoubtedly knows the story, it nonetheless bears repeating: By late 1938, the pulp publishing magnate of Street & Smith was determined to revamp *Astounding Science Fiction* for broader readership. In particular, senior editorial director F. Orlin Tremaine called for stories with a stronger *human element*. When acting editor John W. Campbell balked, preferring his spaceship-driven tales,

Tremaine enlisted Hubbard. Hubbard, in turn, replied with the genre's first truly *character-driven* works, wherein heroes are pitted not against bug-eyed monsters but the mystery and majesty of deep space itself—and thus was launched the Golden Age of Science Fiction.

The names alone are enough to quicken the pulse of any science fiction aficionado, including LRH friend and protégé, Robert Heinlein, Isaac Asimov, A. E. van Vogt and Ray Bradbury. Moreover, when coupled with LRH stories of fantasy, we further come to what's rightly been described as the foundation of every modern tale of horror: L. Ron Hubbard's immortal *Fear*. It was rightly proclaimed by Stephen King as one of the very few works to genuinely warrant that overworked term "classic"—as in: *"This is a classic tale of creeping, surreal menace and horror. . . . This is one of the really, really good ones."*

L. Ron Hubbard, 1948, among fellow science fiction luminaries at the World Science Fiction Convention in Toronto.

To accommodate the greater body of L. Ron Hubbard fantasies, Street & Smith inaugurated *Unknown*—a classic pulp if there ever was one, and wherein readers were soon thrilling to the likes of *Typewriter in the Sky* and *Slaves of Sleep* of which Frederik Pohl would declare: *"There are bits and pieces from Ron's work that became part of the language in ways that very few other writers managed."*

And, indeed, at J. W. Campbell Jr.'s insistence, Ron was regularly drawing on themes from the Arabian Nights and

137

so introducing readers to a world of genies, jinn, Aladdin and Sinbad—all of which, of course, continue to float through cultural mythology to this day.

At least as influential in terms of post-apocalypse stories was L. Ron Hubbard's 1940 *Final Blackout*. Generally acclaimed as the finest anti-war novel of the decade and among the ten best works of the genre ever authored—here, too, was a tale that would live on in ways few other writers

Portland, Oregon, 1943; L. Ron Hubbard captain of the US Navy subchaser PC 815.

imagined. Hence, the later Robert Heinlein verdict: "Final Blackout *is as perfect a piece of science fiction as has ever been written.*"

Like many another who both lived and wrote American pulp adventure, the war proved a tragic end to Ron's sojourn in the pulps. He served with distinction in four theaters and was highly decorated for commanding corvettes in the North Pacific. He was also grievously wounded in combat, lost many a close friend and colleague and thus resolved to say farewell to pulp fiction and devote himself to what it had supported these many years—namely, his serious research.

But in no way was the LRH literary saga at an end, for as he wrote some thirty years later, in 1980:

"Recently there came a period when I had little to do. This was novel in a life so crammed with busy years, and I decided to amuse myself by writing a novel that was pure science fiction."

138

That work was *Battlefield Earth: A Saga of the Year 3000.* It was an immediate *New York Times* bestseller and, in fact, the first international science fiction blockbuster in decades. It was not, however, L. Ron Hubbard's magnum opus, as that distinction is generally reserved for his next and final work: The 1.2 million word *Mission Earth.*

> **Final Blackout**
> *is as perfect a piece of science fiction as has ever been written.*
>
> —**Robert Heinlein**

How he managed those 1.2 million words in just over twelve months is yet another piece of the L. Ron Hubbard legend. But the fact remains, he did indeed author a ten-volume *dekalogy* that lives in publishing history for the fact that each and every volume of the series was also a *New York Times* bestseller.

Moreover, as subsequent generations discovered L. Ron Hubbard through republished works and novelizations of his screenplays, the mere fact of his name on a cover signaled an international bestseller. . . . Until, to date, sales of his works exceed hundreds of millions, and he otherwise remains among the most enduring and widely read authors in literary history. Although as a final word on the tales of L. Ron Hubbard, perhaps it's enough to simply reiterate what editors told readers in the glory days of American Pulp Fiction:

He writes the way he does, brothers, because he's been there, seen it and done it!

THE STORIES FROM THE GOLDEN AGE

Your ticket to adventure starts here with the Stories from the Golden Age collection by master storyteller L. Ron Hubbard. These gripping tales are set in a kaleidoscope of exotic locales and brim with fascinating characters, including some of the most vile villains, dangerous dames and brazen heroes you'll ever get to meet.

The entire collection of over one hundred and fifty stories is being released in a series of eighty books and audiobooks. For an up-to-date listing of available titles, go to www.goldenagestories.com.

AIR ADVENTURE

FAR-FLUNG ADVENTURE

The Adventure of "X"
All Frontiers Are Jealous
The Barbarians
The Black Sultan
Black Towers to Danger
The Bold Dare All
Buckley Plays a Hunch
The Cossack
Destiny's Drum
Escape for Three
Fifty-Fifty O'Brien
The Headhunters
Hell's Legionnaire
He Walked to War
Hostage to Death

Hurricane
The Iron Duke
Machine Gun 21,000
Medals for Mahoney
Price of a Hat
Red Sand
The Sky Devil
The Small Boss of Nunaloha
The Squad That Never Came Back
Starch and Stripes
Tomb of the Ten Thousand Dead
Trick Soldier
While Bugles Blow!
Yukon Madness

SEA ADVENTURE

Cargo of Coffins
The Drowned City
False Cargo
Grounded
Loot of the Shanung
Mister Tidwell, Gunner

The Phantom Patrol
Sea Fangs
Submarine
Twenty Fathoms Down
Under the Black Ensign

TALES FROM THE ORIENT

MYSTERY

143

FANTASY

SCIENCE FICTION

WESTERN